THE FOREIGN NATIONAL

Tori – Thank you so much for the support!

THE FOREIGN NATIONAL

LUCA MCLEOD

NEW DEGREE PRESS

THE FOREIGN NATIONAL

ISBN   978-1-63730-712-0   *Paperback*

            978-1-63730-850-9   *Kindle Ebook*

            979-8-88504-003-7   *Ebook*

CONTENTS

———

AUTHOR'S NOTE

————

Dear foreign nationals, this book is for you.

From the beginning of time, territories have secluded one population from another. We have been taught that everyone within a perimeter belongs to a country, a community of like-minded people, and, more importantly, a big family. Now more than ever, in our highly globalized and diversified world, we know this isn't true, as people from various backgrounds are not treated equally in their own country of residence or origin. While traveling, I have met others who do not possess a sense of pride in their homeland or feel the comfort they wish or expect to have within their birth countries. This has made me wonder how many people can identify with this sense of not belonging. And why is this so?

Maybe it is because other multinationals 1) do not feel solely attached to any single country, as is the case with me, or 2) feel excluded by fellow citizens because of their background. On an even larger scale, maybe it is because they are not treated as first-class citizens because of the color of their skin, their religion, their immigration status, their gender, or any other distinction that makes one "lesser" in some people's eyes.

Despite the many pros of globalization, such as connecting people from all parts of the world, there are also challenges. Because life can take unexpected turns, no matter where you reside, it is vital for all of us to have a sense of community, whether we live in or outside of our birth countries. Identity crises, loss, struggles, hardships, and tragedy are bound to happen, and it's up to us, as fellow citizens, to support each other in times of need. We need to keep pushing one another forward, especially when we feel like we've lost ourselves.

I grew up in Atlanta, London, Barcelona, Koblenz, and I currently live in Miami. I come from a diverse, multiracial background. My mom is white and German, and my dad is half-black and half-white, an American born in the UK. I attended six different schools in twelve years and in four separate countries.

Many people like me find it hard to answer the question, "Where are you from?" There is no easy answer, and people may have a hard time understanding an answer that isn't clear-cut. I am not from any one of the places I mentioned; I am from all of them, and they have all played an enormous role in who I am today.

Despite what I say, in every country I have gone to, I have always been assigned a new nationality. The British kid, the Spaniard, the German, and, on some occasions, the American kid. Because I have been an outsider from an early age, I became more of a listener, observer, and thinker rather than a socializer. Trying to figure out who I am and where I am from has led me down the rabbit hole. I ask myself, *What and who is a foreign national?*

The term "foreign national" does not just apply to people like me who have lived in various countries and don't identify with any of them. Foreign nationals exist within countries, regions, and communities and can even be someone who has never stepped outside their local town. A long history of injustices against foreign nationals has made people feel discriminated against, making them feel foreign in their own country.

In dealing with different environments and treatment, mental health issues can also arise. Foreign nationals are continuously tested, struggling to surround themselves with a good group of people.

The Foreign National follows Marco's story as he and his family work to find a sense of community and success within their career fields as foreign nationals. When Marco experiences life-changing tragedies, he questions his self-worth and this sense of belonging. Through the support of friends and his inner self, he's able to push through his own depression, challenging himself to reach his full potential... before life strikes again.

By reading this book, you'll learn more about a common experience many of us have but do not know how to define or come to peace with. The term "foreign national" is purposefully vague because of the vast range of experiences people have that still reach the same outcomes, namely the desire to be included in a community.

I hope this book inspires you to learn more about different countries, cultures, and people. Every one of us has stories and struggles, and in these tough times, we will hopefully find our inner peace. The backbone of human existence and overcoming challenges is support. Support from the person next to you, from the person below you, and from the person above you. We each play a significant role in making the human race a better community.

CHAPTER 1

—

"This is DFF breaking news."

"Good afternoon. Live from DFF's headquarters in New York City, I'm Carolina Cruz."

"And I'm Jim Holmes. Just moments ago, we were informed that Marco, widely known as the Foreign National, the man who has become one of the most popular people—if not *the* most popular person—on the planet, has gone missing in Bangkok, Thailand!"

"More coming up shortly."

***

MARCO, EARLIER THAT MORNING.

I'm lounging in the Fatboy beanbag chair with my journal flipped open to the entry from a couple of days ago.

It is 5:00 a.m., and I can't seem to fall asleep. Many thoughts are running through my mind, so I decide to open my journal and write under the little bed lamp.

So fun, so cool, so painful, so sad. I am young, but I feel like I have lived many lives. I am twenty-seven years old, to be concrete. What do people my age usually do? Party, get married, get good jobs... what else? I am trying to reinvent myself. I have this dilemma—the more I do, the more I miss. I've been to many places, met a lot of amazing people, learned to some degree or another a decent number of languages. I was doing everything I could until I couldn't anymore.

I don't believe in goodbyes. We'll see each other again, but every time I leave, it takes a little piece of me. It is hard to see little kids wave and smile at me, knowing that a third of them won't even make it to my age. Incredibly hard. I wanted to do everything, but the burden ate me alive. Until I hit rock bottom and almost went under.

Today is a new day. Today I'm seeing my father again. I am a step closer to the end of the tunnel. I see the light.

***

My dad walks out of the arrival terminal.

Must have been a rough flight. There are bags under his eyes. He's slouching a little and looks a bit disoriented. I guess all those years of flying must have finally taken a toll on him.

I hurry to him with a big smile. "It's hard to believe you used to do Ironmans."

"Have you done one in under eleven hours yet?" he shoots back.

"Good one. You still got the quick comebacks, I see!"

We laugh.

"Those never age."

"How was the flight?" I ask him while taking his bag and some of his luggage.

"Longest one I've ever had!"

"Alright, well, make sure you rest up because tomorrow is New Year's Eve."

"All I'm thinking about is bed!"

It's been years since I've seen my dad. The last time was right before I left the States. I needed to escape from everything going on around me and in my head. So I came here. My beloved Thailand.

It was an adjustment. No doubt. But not for the reasons people would expect. Not the language barriers or cultural differences, but the weather. That took some getting used to. Especially the rainy season. It isn't a constant drizzle or a five-minute water dump from the sky. I have lived in places like London, where it rains a lot, and Miami, where it can rain with intensity at any given moment. Thailand and its neighboring countries are different. Plain and simple. They have full-blown rainy seasons, which means it rains literally almost every day.

On the flip side, during the hot season, the average temperature is almost 100°F, and on many days, it will cross that mark. I lived in Miami for six years, but I will never get used to humidity and heat. At least in South Florida during the summertime, there was always a rain shower in the early afternoon to cool things down. Not here.

A couple of months ago, my dad reached out to me because he wanted to come to see me right then and there, but with the rainy season being from July to October, I thought he should wait until at least the end of fall. Instead of him coming immediately like he wanted, I told him to come during the Holiday season because it's beautiful here during that time. After some back-and-forth, I managed to convince him to wait and come in December.

My dad loves parks, and when I was a baby, he would always take me in the stroller on his runs in Piedmont Park in Atlanta. So, after a long night's rest, I decided to take him to the most well-known park in Bangkok.

Off we go.

"What's your running distance these days?" I asked my dad.

"Well, the last several months, not much, but before that, I would try to do four to five miles."

We're jogging already, and I'm surprised at the fact that he doesn't look like he is in good shape.

"That's good! Every day?" I point to the other side of the street so we can get ready to cross.

"As much as I can, but no. It depends on how my body feels."

"Still a lot more than most people your age!" I joke, tapping him on the shoulder.

"Easy with the shoulder!"

"Sorry, it's been a long time," I explain, barely able to contain my excitement. "Here we are! The entrance to Lumpini Park. All of it was man-made."

My dad looks around, impressed. "Nice! How long is the path?"

"About one and a half miles."

"Not too bad. I think Piedmont is about four miles."

"Yeah, I come here every morning. How many laps do you want to do?"

My dad is dressed as if we are about to run an ultramarathon. He's got the long socks and the arm sleeves on. He's got the look.

"I am good with one. Just to stretch my muscles a bit," he says, regardless of his attire.

Wow, okay. That's a shocker.

***

Around 4:00 p.m., I ask, "You ready?"

"Yep," my dad replies as he grabs a pair of nicer shoes from his luggage.

The plan is to take him to try some food from a famous market close by and then show him around the area before we get on a nice boat to celebrate the New Year.

"Alright, let's go and eat. And, just so you know, the market is very big."

"I'm sixty-eight. You don't think I've been to big markets?"

He doesn't understand. These aren't like Western markets.

"The Chatuchak Weekend Market is the biggest market in the world."

"How big is the biggest?"

"Over fifteen thousand booths and more than two hundred thousand visitors every weekend."

"Impressive! And I'm guessing you come here every weekend?" he adds.

"That's right! There is always something new to try."

I come to this market every Saturday just to eat and smell all the great food. When I get full, I walk around until my stomach is ready to eat more, and then the food adventure continues. I have only scratched the surface of everything they have to offer in the few years I've been here.

Today, I am not going to try anything new. I am only taking him to the places I love the most.

This is the menu I have planned out. It's better to try a little bit of many choices than to get full on one thing. A lot of these dishes aren't big, and we're sharing one portion, so we'll be fine.

Appetizers:

- Garlic Bread from Hello Garlic (฿30, $0.99)
- Fried Octopus at King Octopus (฿50–200, $1.65–6.61)

- Honey Roast Pork at Moo Yang Nam Peung (฿50, $1.65)
- Duck Noodle at Drum Stick Duck Noodle (฿50, $1.65)
- Noodle Soup with Chicken at SOI 29 (฿50, $1.65)

Main Entrée:
- Paella at Viva 8 (฿160, $5.29)

Dessert:
- Coconut Ice Cream at Coco JJ (฿60, $1.98)
- Mango Sticky Rice at Mango Sticky Rice Vendor (฿50, $1.65)
- Tub Tim Grob at Tub Tim Grob Shop (฿40, $1.32)

I think he'll love it. In fact, I know he will.

***

My apartment is in the Phra Khanong neighborhood of Bangkok, which is not too far away from the market. It's nothing special, but it's nice and cozy. I let my dad sleep on the bed, and I blow up the air mattress I have since I have friends who stay with me from time to time.

"I've been thinking." I push open the door to exit the building.

"Mm-hmm?"

"It has been four and half years now since I left, and I don't miss the West. I love it here."

"Marco, don't you love every place you go?"

"Yeah, but you know it's different here. I have reinvented myself." I'm happy, energetic, and motivated to live again.

"You do look a lot better. It took me sixty-eight years to come to this part of the world."

"Why did you never come?" I ask him, genuinely curious about his answer.

"There were always so many other places I wanted to go that Asia never caught my interest."

We're almost at the market already. This will certainly catch his attention. Large crowds, walking in the same direction we are, are already starting to form.

"The first stall is a couple of minutes away," I say.

"Is it your favorite one?"

"The ones today are all my favorite." We crack up. "But it is my favorite starter stall."

"Your love for Thai food goes way back."

That confuses me. When did I eat Thai food? "How far back? I don't remember eating Thai food in my childhood."

"Since you were a baby."

"Really?"

"Back in Atlanta, your mom and I took you with us to visit some Thai friends, and while we were chitchatting, we didn't even realize"—my dad starts laughing a bit—"your face was all in the food."

"Thai food?"

"Yeah, authentic Thai food. Spicy too, but you didn't stop eating."

"How old was I?"

"Uh, I think around one or one and a half."

We're two blocks away from the market.

My dad gets distracted by the large number of people around. "Very busy street, huh?"

"Yeah, one of the busiest in Bangkok."

"Reminds me of Oxford Street," he says, reminiscing.

"I remember a little bit from the days when we used to live in London," I say. "The first time I walked here, I was thinking the same exact thing."

"I remember one time… you must have been around five years old… the five of us were walking down Oxford Street." We weave around a few people. "I had your sister on my back and you by the hand. Your mom absolutely wanted me to hold you by the hand. She would have killed me otherwise."

"Yep, she would." My mom always liked to have us close.

"And she would hold your brother's hand."

"Oxford Street is special!" I understand parents don't like that street, but as a kid, I loved it. The huge stores and all the adults. Absolutely cool.

"For tourists, it is! We took you guys only a few times down that street. Just too busy for our taste."

"Well, I loved that street because it had the best toy store in the world!"

"Hamleys?"

"Yep, Hamleys. Absolute heaven."

I would dream of that place. It had the most amazing things any kid could ever want.

***

We're at the Garlic Bread stall. Best garlic bread, in my opinion, and my dad likes it a lot too.

"This is a nice market!" my dad says.

"I knew you would like it."

"You know, everywhere I would go, people would always ask me what they needed to do to live the adventurous life I was living," he says.

Uh, I wonder what he said. Break up with your partner? Quit your job? Drop out of school?

"What did you tell them?"

"Go for it! Simple. Go for it!"

"That's simple."

"It is, but they would always say they couldn't because of another person or job or whatever other excuse."

"People love ideas and dreams," I say.

But acting on them is risky because you can get disappointed. Dreams never disappoint because you imagine perfection.

"It's a pity. People miss out on a lot."

"Too bad Mom couldn't come." I miss her a lot.

"Yeah, she would have loved it. When you were young, for many years, we would drop you off at Opi's and Omi's and then go to a different big city for New Year's Eve."

"Bangkok is way different from any other place you two have gone to."

"I agree."

Now, we are in the part of the market with the most people. There isn't much of a walking path, and many of the stalls lean into this space. I zigzag through people, trying to find holes to get through. We get split up, and my dad is quite distant ahead of me.

I see him turn around, looking for me. "Marco?"

He can't see me. I want to answer, but someone covers my mouth.

"Marco!" He raises his voice.

Struggling against the unwelcome grip, I feel my eyes closing and my head getting dizzy. The next thing I know, I am in a dark place. I cannot see anything, and I have no clue where I am. I hear footsteps approaching...

Then I'm gone.

CHAPTER 2

SIXTEEN YEARS EARLIER.

"Good evening, and welcome to DFF. My name is Jeff."

"And I'm Karen. Today's story stars an eleven-year-old, self-made millionaire whose website has revolutionized the way middle school and high school students interact with each other beyond the school premises."

"That's right, Karen. This platform is a social media page that extends the classroom and school environment to the internet. Students can easily interact with each other individually or with the classroom. They can create study groups and share their fun moments with their schoolmates or with students all over the world."

"What an incredible story this is. It's hot right now, and parents love it too!"

"More about that shortly."

***

EARLIER THAT DAY.

"Are you ready?" I impatiently ask my dad.

"Five minutes, Marco," my dad says while he pours the coffee in a cup.

Today is one of those perfect Sundays to go to the L'Illa Mall, one of Barcelona's most famous shopping centers. It's raining, and I already finished all of my homework. My dad can buy a book he's been wanting to read, and I can get some food afterward from Central Café. They have some awesome sandwiches and special sweet tea with fresh fruit.

The Fnac in the L'Illa is everyone's favorite place to buy books in Barcelona. I am a big fan, too, not for the same reasons as my dad, but because of the Apple products and the international literature genre section. This is where I find my happiness. I sometimes get novels and workbooks in random languages and try to figure them out as I go. It's a lot of fun.

They have all different genres, but they only have a small section for English and an even smaller section of other languages. My dad's Spanish isn't the best, so he sticks to the English ones. My siblings and I always make fun of his Spanish.

One time, we were at the entrance of our tennis club, Sanchez-Casals, and he realized he had forgotten the membership card to get past the gate.

He rolled down the window and said to the security guard, "*No tengo la taheta.*" (I don't have the card.)

"*Tarjeta, not taheta,*" my brother said.

Everybody laughed except my dad. "Do *you* want to speak to him?"

"No, no. I am just trying to help you. *Tarrrrjeta.*"

Funny moments. Anyway, back to the books. English ones only!

My dad and I play this little game. As soon as we're close to Fnac, I usually run to the English section, pick out the ones I think he will like, and by the time he gets to me, I hand him my findings. For every one he decides to buy, I get one euro worth of sweets at the candy store. He's really into the apocalyptic genre, especially Jo Nesbo's work, so anytime I see a new one from Nesbo, I know I have some guaranteed sweets.

***

L'Illa is about twenty-five minutes away from home, and we are ready to leave the house.

"Can I sit in the front?" I ask hopefully. I enjoy sitting in the front, but he doesn't always let me.

"Yep," my dad says.

I jump in, and off we go.

"So, at Victor's house the other day, I was thinking about what else we can do." I always get excited when I share my ideas with my dad.

"For the website?"

"Yes. So I have two ideas."

I enjoy connecting with people everywhere, and I really want to reach as many students in the world as possible. I was born in Washington, DC, but I have lived in a couple of countries already, including France, Japan, and now Spain. All of this is because my dad is a US diplomat. I might want to do that job too when I get older, although he does work a lot of hours.

Education has been a big passion of mine for a couple of years now. When I was nine, and we were living in Japan, my dad took me on a trip to Myanmar. We went into the countryside because my dad and some others were meeting with local government officials. While they were busy, I played at the school with the other kids, and I was shocked because those schools were nothing like the ones I had been to. These "buildings" were little huts with no classroom materials and no chairs to sit on, so everyone just sat on the floor. That is when I knew my goal was for every student to have a great education.

"Okay," my dad says, breaking me out of my thoughts.

"First, we should get schools involved, like the director, um… what's her name again?"

"Mother Montserrat?"

"Yes, that's her name." She's actually a really cool nun, old but fun, always smiling, and sometimes, she even comes out to the playground and will play with the students for a little bit. A forward-thinking person, she is originally from Argentina, and she has traveled a lot.

"Are you going to talk to her, Marco?"

"No, no, no. I'm too nervous. You should do it."

He wants *me* to talk to the director of the school? That's too much. I would probably look funny as an eleven-year-old sitting in what is probably a beautiful and huge office.

"No, you got this. I know she'll at least listen to you."

We're driving into a tunnel now. I like how it gets dark all of a sudden. I always wonder if, on the other end is a magical land with all the different kinds of great food in the world. I love food, and people like me for it. They know they can always count on me to eat the whole plate.

"So, how do I make this talk happen?" I ask.

"I'll set up the meeting."

Meeting? Sounds formal.

"Okay…" I hesitantly agree.

"But overall, I like this idea a lot. In business, you will see many companies and organizations making partnerships with others to grow."

"Like Apple for the iPhone?"

I have the iPod Touch, and it is amazing. I hijacked it and now have all the games I want, but hijacking software and Apple are not a partnership. The people involved in making these devices are.

"Exactly, because to make the iPhone, Apple has many partnerships with companies all over the world that help it come together," my dad clarifies.

Ah! I am not thinking globally, but that is a great idea. I was just thinking about local schools.

"So we need partnerships?" I suggest.

"Not just any, but yes, some. And talking to directors and schools would be good from an insights-gathering perspective too."

"What does *insights* mean?" I ponder out loud.

"It's a fancier word for learning something."

"Oh, okay, so yeah. By talking to them, we can learn a lot."

"Exactly! Just like you did when we first started, but now with different people."

How did this website thing begin? I think back. My entrepreneurial start came when I went to the Apple store on Fifth Avenue on a summer vacation trip to New York. My dad was working there for a few weeks, and he took us with him. I already liked Apple before, but after that experience, I became a bigger fan of the brand and wanted to start a business around their products. Have my own store with Apple stuff and other cool things. So I shared my ideas with my dad last summer while he was enjoying his bath, and then he told me this.

"Let me tell you an idea I have, and let me know what you think."

"Okay," I told him, thinking this sounded interesting.

"We need to connect the students, schools, internet, and social media in a better way than anything else out there can, but with something that still has some of these components."

"We use Moodle in school…" I offered, although that is by far my least favorite application we use.

"Does anyone like Moodle?"

"No. And it doesn't have any social media."

"So we need to create Facebook for students and schools. The five components are students, school, internet, social media, and the world."

"Oh, wow, I like that a lot!"

"And *you* are the CEO."

"What's that?" I asked.

"The leader of the company."

"Me? The leader? It's your idea."

"Yes, but you are the one doing the work, and you are the one in charge of how everything goes."

"So, what do I have to do?"

"First thing you need to do is research. You need to get a good understanding of your audience."

I always liked researching.

"And my audience is the students?" I clarified.

"Yes."

"But I already know them."

"You think you do, but you really don't until you have done all the research."

"So, what do I do first?"

"Talk to your classmates. Do a little interview with them," he explains.

"Okay, one second. Before we go further, I want to figure out the questions I should ask them."

"Well, remember that this is the first round. The questions for this one will be kind of generic. For example—actually, get a piece of paper and write these down."

I grabbed my little notebook I take with me everywhere.

Once I was ready, my dad continued slowly, "One question could be, how much time do you spend doing homework? Another one could be, do you do homework by yourself or do you get help? If you get help, is it frequent, somewhat frequent, or rarely?"

"I got one. How do you study?"

"Yep, and to follow up on that one, you could ask if they have a tutor outside of school."

"I have a few more," I exclaimed, feeling inspired. "Do you use the internet for schoolwork? Do you reach out to friends for help with schoolwork? Would you like to have study groups online?"

"That's good enough for the first round. Simple questions. Just tell them it's for a project you're working on."

At first, I was nervous about interviewing my peers, but after a while, it became fun. Every class break, I would interview more of my friends, and at one point, a bunch of students from other classes volunteered to be interviewed too. At the end of the day, once I was done with my homework, I spent hours upstairs in the family office trying to learn as much as possible from the interview answers and from Google.

Early in the process, my dad and I would do a little debrief once or twice a week, just to see where things were at. In the beginning, it was either at the end of the week or after a few days, but now it had kind of blown up. We talked about it all the time.

***

It's amazing to see how far I've come since then, but still, talking to adults is a whole different story than talking to people my age.

"School administrations would be excellent partnerships. They could help us improve our schoolwork and study group features and other functionalities," my dad says.

I think he likes to put me in positions I feel uncomfortable in.

Overall, this conversation is going great, and I think it's time to move on to my second item. "My next idea is what I call 'reflection stories.' Ideally, students will write reflection stories based on one or more events in their life or what they see or read about, and then they tie it together with a learning outcome."

Even though I am only eleven, I have already learned a lot about life from moving around and meeting different people. That has always been important for my parents—making new experiences. I begin brainstorming an example of a reflection story. Perhaps a student has trouble readjusting to a new school or new culture.

"Like a blog?" my dad asks.

"Yes, but not just in written form. Could be a video."

"And what are you trying to get out of these reflection stories, Marco?"

"Well, I want to have a platform for students to share the challenges they're having or how they overcame them."

"An outlet for awareness?"

"Yeah, basically, and since these students are all over the world, I think it would be interesting to read other people's stories from a similar age. You know each of us has stories, and we need to understand what these stories mean to each of us. The best way to build confidence and self-esteem is knowing who you are, and again, that's hard to figure out when you're young."

"That sounds like a complex and big task."

"That is why I think narrowing it down to one or a couple of significant events can help us make sense out of it through learning. Many of us are vulnerable, and my goal is to bring awareness to the stories of young people. I want to understand what others are going through and support them," I finish, glancing at my dad.

My dad smiles silently. "This is… it's really good. Another great idea! I wish I had thought like you when I was your age. Both ideas are great, Marco."

From the beginning, my dad has been the best consultant and supporter anyone could ask for. He will generally tell me what I need to work on without giving me too much information, so I still have to decide how to do the work, do it, and learn along the way. But, for the most part, he'll let me implement my ideas, or we'll have a discussion, and he will make me realize my idea is maybe not the best.

He is the one who had the idea to start with. I would have absolutely not been able to run with it without his guidance and support. When I'm down, he lifts me up. When there's a reason to be happy, we celebrate. Overall, it's been a fun adventure, and my dad constantly pushes me to think outside of the box.

I want to see where this goes, but I do have big dreams. Anyway, we arrive at the mall. It's time to get some candy money.

CHAPTER 3

———

A YEAR LATER.

"Marco is in the hospital!" I faintly hear my dad telling my mom over the phone.

"What?" she yells, a mixture of confusion and worry filling her voice.

"Yes, we are at the hospital ten minutes away…"

I fall asleep.

LATER THAT DAY.

I slowly wake up in what I realize is a hospital bed. The anesthesia wears off little by little, and my brother stands next to my bed. Even though we compete a lot, we also have a lot of respect and love for each other. I wonder what he is thinking. For the most part, James is a happy person, but he doesn't seem to be feeling that way now. My parents notice I am waking up, and my dad gets up from his chair and sidles over to me with a big smile on his face. He signals to my brother and my sister to go to my Mom. She presses some money into their hands, and both James and Maria leave the room.

"What's up, Marco?" my dad asks gently.

I try to smile back, but my body feels a little bit nauseated from the medication. "I don't know. I should ask you that question," I joke, finally managing a small grin.

I notice some heaviness on my left forearm, and as I shift my head over, I see a lot of bandages. What happened?

Oh.

"How long will I need all of this?" I ask, studying my bandages.

"Doctors said about a week or so. It needs to fully heal before you take it off," my mom answers from the back of the room.

I've broken some bones on that same arm—my wrist—in the past. A couple of years ago, I also broke my ring finger on my right hand. That time I was playing soccer. I was the goalie, and my hand was right in front of the crossbar when the ball hit it. No gloves, so no protection whatsoever. That was painful, and I instantly knew I was going to make a trip to the hospital that afternoon and that they were going to pull my finger. This time, though, I was in the hospital for a different reason.

"How do you feel, Marco?" my mom asks me, concerned.

I can tell she spent some time crying. As I am wondering what the doctor told her, someone knocks on the door and turns the handle to open it.

"I hear someone is awake," a manly voice announces. "Hey, Marco. My name is Dr. Johnson," he introduces himself as he approaches the bed. With such a potent voice, I would not have imagined him to be five and a half feet tall.

"Hello, Dr. Johnson."

"How are you feeling?" he asks as he examines me.

"Good, but tired."

"Yes, I can imagine. The meds are probably still wearing off. Soon you won't feel the side effects anymore."

I weakly smile and nod.

"Just so you know, I spoke to your parents earlier"—he glances at them before continuing—"and you are going to spend the night here. We need to do some testing, and that will be done in the morning once you feel better. That way, we can provide you with what you need, and then you'll be good to go." He grins a little too widely.

This is definitely the most energetic doctor I have ever met. Powerful voice and a lot of positive emotions. He should run for president.

"One of us will stay with you, Marco," my mom says, trying to comfort me.

"Okay," I agree, although I am doing perfectly fine.

"Awesome. I will check in on you later, Marco, but if you need anything, let the nurse know, and I will come."

"Thanks, Dr. Johnson."

"Your food should be coming any moment now too, and from what I hear, today's food is delicious."

I laugh. "Thank you!"

My dad smiles and nods.

I look at my parents as the doctor leaves the room. "Why am I spending the night here? There's nothing else they can do to my arm. It just has to heal."

"Dr. Johnson wants you to go through some tests and speak to a psy—"

My mom cuts my dad off. "Marco, are you depressed?" She's visibly sad and looks like she could start crying again at any moment.

I don't say anything. I don't know what depression really is. I've heard of it, but I don't know if that is what I have.

My dad leans against the bed. "You know, I went through something I never told you about because your mom was afraid that it would..."

I look in his direction.

"Um, instigate it, I guess," he continues. "Depression runs in the family, specifically my family."

His voice sounds full of guilt and sadness at the same time.

What a funny time to tell me this, while I'm in the hospital.

But in either case, he has my full attention. I'm wide awake now.

"Are you telling me you are depressed?" I ask him.

I look past my dad, and I see a tear going down my mom's face.

"Not anymore," he answers. "One of the things I am most thankful about your mom is that she got me into therapy. I didn't go soon enough..."

"Because it's not cool? Or because men don't do that?"

"I grew up in the seventies, in a generation that didn't believe in therapy. Therapy was only for crazy or seriously mentally ill people," my dad explained.

"Isn't depression considered a serious mental issue, though?"

"Yes, and I should have gone much sooner. What I am trying to say, though, is that your mom and I are here for you. We will get through this together."

I do not respond. Instead, I look at the door, waiting for my food. I hear some footsteps coming close.

Knock, knock.

My food is here. The nurse also gives me some Malta, a lightly carbonated, nonalcoholic malt beverage brewed from barley, hops, and water. The last time I had it was in the hospital in England, and I liked it, so I'm happy to accept it.

***

The next morning, I do various tests, speak to a psychiatrist, and she prescribes me some antidepressants and therapy sessions a couple of times a week. By four o'clock in the afternoon, I am back at home.

Now is the time. I'm at the family office, and I ask my parents and siblings if they need to use it in the next couple of hours, and they all say no. Good, because I have a lot to think about and write in my journal that I recently bought, even with all these bandages around my writing arm.

I have time. I take a deep breath and blow out the air. Alright!

***

Exactly a week ago, I remember thinking that I wanted to hurt myself badly and relieve myself from everything I was keeping inside. This all happened while my parents and siblings weren't at home. I think my dad was with my brother at a soccer game, my mom was with my sister somewhere else, and I decided to stay at home and think about the business, or maybe even nothing at all. I don't remember anymore.

I don't know why, but I felt a mixture of emotions. I was sad, angry, frustrated, and confused all at the same time. I wanted to let it all out. In the end, I decided to cut myself with no intention of ending up in the hospital, but… things turned out worse than I thought.

Did I feel any better? Yes, I felt great! Cutting myself was the best thing that could have ever happened to me. It was the first time people around me finally understood what was going on without needing words. I now finally understand what I have been going through, and I have an answer to a question I was too afraid to ask.

Now that I know the term for what I have been going through, I can say I've been depressed for years, and I never knew. It was so normal to me that I learned to live with it. I feel great, energetic, and ready to help the world become a better place at times. And then I have phases when I feel sad for no reason, and I don't want to do anything. I've been able to hide it because I would always find ways to still get homework and other things done. I didn't socialize much, and when I had to put on a fake smile, I would. I know how to play the game.

This past month was different. We moved again, this time to Buenos Aires. I don't know why, but it was overwhelming for me to leave and say goodbye to my friends this time. I have also been feeling stressed because of all the things that come with running a fast-growing website… more than my parents and I could have ever imagined. But with tremendous growth comes tremendous expectations, and I would spend a lot of time analyzing feedback, coming up with new ideas, speaking to my dad and other people on the team, talking to our partners, and on and on. These last three weeks, I have also had my end of the year exams. It is not like these tests will decide where I go to college. I'm only in middle school, but still, I want to do well in everything.

Leaving school wasn't an option because my mom would never in a million years let that happen. She is an academic, and even the thought of her son not finishing school would probably give her a heart attack. I like being around people anyway because working alone all day in front of a screen sounds too much for me.

In the last couple of months, I would more frequently sit and daydream for I don't know how long, and my parents wouldn't even notice. I think my body would sometimes temporarily shut down.

During lunch breaks, while everybody is outside playing after eating, I would sneak back into the classroom and stay there until about five minutes before the bell, and then I would go outside. I would sit in the classroom and stare straight ahead.

It's 8:30 p.m., and it is time to write my one paragraph. Word of the day: *alone.*

I am twelve, and I have already been to a bunch of different schools with completely different education systems. Sometimes I feel (and it is true on some occasions) that the various student groups don't want to accept me. But when I think about it now, I realize that I also would alienate myself sometimes and maybe even oftentimes. I do not try to join groups or make close friendships. Two years ago, when I was in fifth grade in Barcelona, the teacher decided to do a class exercise that consisted of describing a classmate in one word as a class. The word my classmates came up with for me was antisocial. It didn't bother me that they chose that word. I don't think I even understood what that word meant.

"Marco, you need to eat something. It's nine o'clock!" my mom yells at me from downstairs.

Wow, time flies by fast.

"Coming."

To be continued, I glumly think.

CHAPTER 4

CAMP NOU FOR EL CLÁSICO (BARÇA VS. MADRID). A COUPLE MONTHS AFTER THE HOSPITAL VISIT.

"Goal!"

Everybody jumps up and celebrates the fifth goal. Wow, this is unbelievable! *Five* goals. This must be a dream. Jeffrén scores this time, and with that, Barcelona absolutely killed Madrid with a five to zero score.

"*Que paliza,*" my mom tells me. *What a beating.*

"Jeffrén! Jeffrén! Jeffrén!" the crowd sings along.

Piqué raises his hand to the crowd with his fingers extended. *La manita*, the handful Barça just served Madrid, wraps up this magical game.

***

TWO DAYS EARLIER.

My parents bought this huge Fatboy, and I love to sit on it and think about everything. With a couple days left until the two soccer teams fight to the last minute to prove who is the best, I am looking forward to being among ninety thousand people cheering for Barça. Among crowds, you will find people from all different backgrounds experiencing many of the same emotions in live-action. But once you step out of that stadium, you are the minority again. This, along with the great teamwork we see from good teams, is what I want to write about in my journal now.

First things first, I am a huge FC Barcelona fan, so when I talk about soccer, I am biased in their favor, but few people would disagree with the point that their great success in recent years is mainly due to their almost flawless teamwork.

So what is a team? You stick a bunch of people together with some glue, and that's it? People with chemistry? Proximity? Association? People that can count on each other in dire moments? Ride-or-die people?

Teams form, grow, flourish, and—unfortunately often in sports—eventually fall as well. Being at the top forever is impossible because better squads will expose the faults of previously great ones. The cycle repeats.

Like any other species on Earth, we can't survive alone. We depend on a support network. Whether it is parents, other caregivers, friends, coworkers, a significant other, sports teammates, or any other people we encounter in life, we need them. Their assistance is fundamental to our existence, but we can be selfish and only care about our own needs.

I gaze up from my writing when I realize this is where I have been failing. Because I moved around a lot, I created my self-aid system and didn't allow others to support me.

I will not be around these people for long anyway, I always thought, *So why bother?*

This is not a good way to approach life, and neither is it healthy in the long term.

Throughout history, people from different backgrounds have separated people into us and them. Think of racism and sexism as examples. It begins as a psychological difference that naturally then justifies a physical one. If we look at segregation in the United States, it started with the white belief that black people were inferior. As a result, they segregated bathrooms, water fountains, playgrounds, bus seating, and neighborhoods.

Few activities in the world can work magic on false preconceived notions like sports. Sports bring out passion in people, unlike any other human activity. This passion transcends other tensions (e.g., racial or cultural) and temporarily illuminates the beauty of our species before the light dims and the night goes on.

Sports bring us together. They are fun to play, exciting to watch, and help people from all walks of life socialize. Some sports are played and viewed more than others, but the end result is the same—people coming together to encourage their players or team. In Argentina, like in many other countries, soccer is the most famous sport.

For a lot of people, soccer changes their whole attitude toward life. When I was still in Spain, the country won its first World Cup, and, at least to me, people seemed so much happier. They forgot about the economic crisis and all the other challenges in the country. It's like when you finally get a splinter out of your foot. The relief is unexplainable... the air is lighter. Our attitude dictates our life. In Spain and many other places, people breathe soccer. It's their oxygen line. Some of these people have been waiting for fifty, sixty, or seventy years to say they are World Cup champions.

Soccer is like a second partner to many. If the team is playing up to the viewers' expectations, then they are happy, excited, and in love. Overall, the relationship is going well. If they are not playing up to par, there is some tension, frustration, anger, and shakiness in the relationship.

I think we inherently want to root for someone and something, even if we don't realize it. We are social beings, so that predisposition comes out in unexpected ways.

The by-product of that theory is that by siding with a person or a group, we often unintentionally and naturally view other people as opponents. On a lower level, we might not care about athletes on opposing squads, but we feel strong hate toward them in some cases. And yet—interestingly—the moment a player from a rival lineup switches and joins yours, your whole perception of that person takes a 180. All of a sudden, we become their biggest fan and number one cheerleader.

We don't necessarily hate the player. We hate who they were playing for. That is the root of most problems humankind has ever faced. We don't view the person as they are. Instead, we see who they represent. Here's an analogy in our society. When a person from a specific race or ethnicity "joins" or socializes more with another one, certain people of that other race may not like this person because of who they represent. But because this person joined and adopted their way of life, this person is accepted. In the case of a racist, they will say that person "is not one of us."

Satisfied with my entry, I set my pencil down and close my journal. I am getting excited about this game. I've been to one before, but I was little, and I have only one memory from that game, Brazilian Ronaldo missing a 1–1 opportunity to score. Barcelona versus Madrid is the biggest soccer rivalry in the world. Historically, these two have had a lot of conflicts with each other, which is normal, but lately, it has been even more intense.

***

A WEEK BEFORE THE GAME.
"Where are you, Marco?" asks my dad.

"I am in the kitchen," I mumble while eating a *polvorón* and a little bit of *turrón de jijona*.

In the winter, we always have traditional foods. I like the *polvorones* and the *turron* the most. Both of them are sweet. A *polvorón* is a thick, soft, crumbly cookie. *Turrón* is a nougat confection shaped into a rectangular tablet. The main ingredient in both of them is nuts.

My dad walks into the kitchen. "My company just called me, and they need me to go to London next week. The flight is for this Sunday."

"So what about the game," I say, more of a statement than a question.

"I just spoke to Mom, and she will take you guys."

Typical. Especially since my hospitalization and his confession, things haven't been the same between my dad and me, in a bad way.

"But when I come back on Friday," he continues, pulling me out of my thoughts, "I want to take you out."

"Okay." I guess he wants to have a chitchat. Anyway, I'm done eating my sweets and have no reason to stay in the kitchen. I wipe my hands on my pants and stalk out without another word to my dad.

My mom takes all of us in the end, and it works out because my sister is short enough to go in as a free guest and sit on my mom's lap.

***

NOVEMBER 29: GAME DAY.

We are waiting in the car for my sister's dance practice to end. It ends at 7:00 p.m., and the start time for the game is 8:00 p.m. Kind of tight to make it on time, but at least her practice isn't too far from the stadium.

"Can I get a *bocadillo de lomo* at the stadium?" I ask my mom.

"Yes, Marco," she replies absentmindedly, watching out the front window for my sister. I can tell she's eager to get going too.

"Me too," my brother says.

"Yes, you too."

I feel like my mom isn't even listening. She has turned her attention to her phone now.

"And sweets?"

At this point, she is annoyed we're still asking her questions. She is busy reading through her emails. "You guys can share one small bag of sweets, and that's it! Your father wouldn't let you have any sweets, and you know it."

Great, we will get what we want. "Thank you," I say, satisfied with the result.

I see my sister running toward us out of the building.

"There she is."

My mom turns around. "Alright, give her the clothes behind you so she can change in here."

At that moment, rain begins pelting the car's roof with heavy, thick drops.

"Oh, no. Can one of you look in the back and see if there is an umbrella too?"

"Here are the clothes, but I don't see an umbrella," my brother responds.

"Check under the seats."

"Nope, nothing," he replies, making her frown.

"Marco, do you know if we're under the roof on that side of the stadium?"

"I don't know, but I don't think so. I guess we'll see."

"If not, we're getting wet," she challenges with a shrug. I hope she doesn't think I'm willing to skip the game because of a little rain.

"We'll be fine," I say.

"Hey, Maria," my mom greets my sister as she piles into the car, wet from the unexpected downpour.

"Hey, Mommy," Maria replies while shaking her hair out like a dog.

"How was practice?" My mom doesn't even flinch as water splatters against her face.

"We had a *lot* of new steps to learn," Maria explains as she passes her training bag to us in the back. Then she adds, "Today was the first day of the new choreography we're going to perform in May."

"That's amazing! That's the one where everybody can watch you, right?" says my mom with a big smile.

"Yeah, a lot of people. It's at a place where they have big performances."

"That's awesome, Maria!" says my mom in a motherly fashion.

"They have a lot of famous people come to that place, too."

My mom is still parked and shows no signs of moving.

"Please, let's go! Can't we talk while we are driving there?" I ask.

"Yes, yes, yes. No rush. We will get there, Marco."

"I know we'll get there, but I want to get there before eight."

One of the most special moments at every Barça game is when their anthem starts. I get goosebumps every time because that's when the players come out. Every person squints and stares, looking hard, trying to spot them. The excitement that comes with that gets me every time.

"Where are we going to park?" I ask.

"By the Sofia Hotel," my mom says as she starts the engine and pulls out of the parking spot.

I've been in that hotel once before briefly. It's a five-star. Nice. "Okay. You think there is parking there?"

"Let's hope so. If not, we have to go a little farther away."

Yeah, I really do hope so.

This game is humongous, and I don't want to miss a single bit of it. You got Messi, Iniesta, Xavi, Dani Alves, Puyol, and Valdes, with Guardiola as the coach. And then with Madrid, you have Cristiano, Benzema, Özil, Marcelo, Xabi Alonso, Ramos, and Casillas, with Mourinho as the coach. Talk about historical lineups.

***

We couldn't find parking by the Sofia, but we didn't have to go far from it.

We're located toward the corner of the stadium, left of where the club presidents sit, thirty seats away from sitting under the cover. I can't complain though; it's a Clásico. I'll let rain fall on me any day of the week to watch this amazing rivalry. Generally, it also adds some extra excitement. We missed most of the anthem, but at least we're on time to watch from the beginning. Let's see who is in the benches down there...

Fast-forwarding to halftime, Barcelona has been dominating Madrid all game. The score is 2–0 when it could have been more. Teamwork at its finest.

Second half now. It's the seventieth minute, and Mourinho still has not left his seat, which is unusual for a coach. Normally, they run up and down their section of the sideline, screaming at players on the other side of the field and waving their hands all over the place. But David Villa just scored two goals about ten minutes ago, so I guess he gave up.

A chant is becoming louder and louder. By the time I could clearly hear it, I was already laughing.

It goes like this: *"Mourinho, sal del banquillo, sal del banquilloooooo."*

This translates into: "Mourinho, leave the bench, leave the beeeench."

My brother and I sing along with our little kid voices. *"Mourinho, sal del banquillo, sal del banquilloooo."*

My mom smiles, and my sister can't wait to leave. She's not impressed at all, and she's cuddled in my mom's lap.

Not even five minutes later, a chant for Cristiano becomes even bigger than the Mourinho one. All game, Cristiano hasn't created much action, let alone gotten any goals.

I can hear it now. My brother and I are laughing even more this time.

My mom tells my sister, "Close your ears."

My sister doesn't even say no. The stadium is too loud for her.

This chant is a little explicit. It goes like this: "*Ese por-togués, hijo puta es,*" which translates into, "That Portuguese son of a bitch he is." It doesn't translate that well into English, but in Spanish, it rhymes. Now imagine more than ninety thousand people singing this.

***

The next morning, I'm sitting back on the Fatboy with my journal flipped open to my entry from a couple of days ago. Yesterday's game was more incredible than I could imagine, and I was thrilled at the teamwork we all had the honor of witnessing. If only we could see that same level of support throughout the rest of the world. If only what you brought to the game mattered as much as your skin color. Suddenly, I have inspiration for today's entry.

Five to zero! I witnessed history. Today, I saw one group of players flourish and another one fall. Great squads, however, are resilient. Madrid will come back sooner than later and stronger. Not every fall is definitive, just like not every victory dictates a great future.

The support system and competitiveness will bring them back up and push them to do better. Just like I see athletes and fans consoling each other after a tough loss (e.g., after a World Cup loss) or lifting each other's heads up, humans, in general, have to do that daily.

I am learning every day how to be a better colleague of humanity—how to emphasize other people's successes and how to make them feel better.

In sports, we often see what should happen in other areas of life but don't. Yes, we have "mini" teams, but I don't want to forget about the one above all, and that is the entirety of human society. So every day is another opportunity for me to do my part in making this world a better one.

People are starving, dying, getting discriminated against, and getting raped, so we have to take care of the people around us—and I mean everyone. Not just the people we care about.

CHAPTER 5

————

Four days later, it's Friday, and my dad is coming back to Barcelona tonight from London. Unlike every other time, I'm not going with my mom to pick him up from the airport. I decided to hang out with some friends and Victor invited me to stay the night at his house. I've been there many times before, and I always have a great time.

Around 5:00 p.m., which is when class always ends for the day, Victor, some other friends, and I head to the soccer field close by and play for a couple hours, even though I prefer tennis.

"Marco," Victor says, getting my attention before lightly kicking the ball to me. "Are you sure your mom is cool with you missing the trip to the airport?"

"I guess. She didn't seem upset," I reply, hoping that's true. I don't know what else to say, so I give the ball a hard kick and watch as everyone starts chasing it and the game begins.

If anything, I am the one who should be upset, and that is why I am here.

***

It's the next day, and I'm looking forward to speaking to my dad. I'm hurt, disappointed, and angry with him. Not for having his own set of mental battles, but for the fact that he never reached out to let me know I wasn't dealing with depression alone. That he, too, knew how it felt. But regardless, I'm ready to speak to him. It's been over a month now, and the more time that passes, the more pain I feel. I can't hold it in any longer.

We're at the L'Illa, and we're eating at Central Café. Today, I don't have much of an appetite.

"Why didn't you tell me?" I suddenly ask my dad, changing the topic of whatever he was going on about. I'm tired of the small talk and frustrated that we've been dancing around the reason I even decided to come.

He puts his spoon down, knowing this conversation was coming. "I couldn't find a good moment to do so."

"Were you ever going to tell me, or was this always supposed to be a secret?" I already know the answer, but I want him to admit it. "For years, I have struggled with it—and also struggled to hide it—and I didn't even know what it was. And then you tell me while I'm lying in a hospital bed that all this time, you were hiding something from me that would have answered all my questions." As I am speaking, I feel myself getting angrier. I notice a few people turning their heads toward us, probably wondering what's going on. Maybe it would have been better to go to a place with fewer people around.

"I agree with you, Marco," he calmly says.

Usually, I like his calmness, but not now.

"But sometimes," he continues, "and you will see this as you grow up… sometimes the most important things to talk about are often the hardest. Do you remember last summer when you asked me why some victims of domestic violence stay in the relationship? I don't know the answer to that, but so many delicate factors go into a decision like that, and only people with shared experiences can understand this. Nobody else can. Because from the outside looking in, everybody has the same thinking as you do."

I feel like he is just trying to avoid the issue. *Stay on topic!*

"This has nothing to do with those people because you are not being domestically abused!" I shout.

"True. I never told you about my mental struggles because that was a dark period in my life I believed I had left behind. A past I did not want to relive because certain things have, um, happened in my life that I never want you to go through. I've always wanted to protect you from those things."

Blah blah blah. Protect me from what? All he has been doing is causing me more pain, frustration, and anger. I have had enough!

"Even though you don't want to think back, do you realize your decision to keep this from me, to 'protect' me, has made my life a living hell for years? I had absolutely no clue what was happening to me and only found relief through cutting myself. I was so frustrated that I felt this way and couldn't explain it, especially because everything else in my life was going so great. You could have helped me deal with it all."

My dad has great emotional intelligence. He knows when to speak, when not to, when to behave in certain ways, and how to read the situation.

"I realize my mistake, Marco. When I saw you bleeding, I saw my younger self. I saw a flashback, and I felt the blood rushing through my body. It brought everything back to me."

For the first time in my life, he looks like someone who knows he is wrong and accepts it.

He continues, "One day, when you have kids, if you decide to have kids, you'll see that even with your best intentions, you'll mess up. And that is what I did. I really messed up this time because I know exactly what you were going through, and, in my case, I didn't get help till much later."

Why is he still trying to justify himself? If I had died, would he have justified that too with *his best intentions*?

"You know, Marco, as a child, we see things in our parents that we like and don't like, and we tell ourselves to do better than them when it is our turn to be a parent. Everyone tells themselves that, and it is good."

I look to my left, and I see a happy family. They're laughing even though the little baby just spat the food out on the dad.

"My father just fulfilled the stereotypical role," my dad states, bringing my attention back. "He worked, he put food on the table, we slept under a roof, and he punished us when we didn't behave. He didn't spend much time with my siblings and me. He would often come home drunk and argue with my mom."

What difference does that make? Clearly, none, because I still ended up in the hospital.

He pauses for a while before pushing forward. "I didn't want to be that type of father. I wanted to be open with you and talk. To play games with you, have fun with you, and support you. When I held you in my arms for the first time, my only goal was to be someone you could always talk to. I think over the years we have achieved that, but I obviously came up short, and—"

"How would you feel if I had died?" I interject.

My dad, a little bit surprised by this, wasn't expecting me to jump in.

"I know you are mad at me, but trust me, I am even more mad at myself. When I was twenty-eight, I was on the verge of killing myself a couple of times, and I would have actually done it the last time I tried."

"What do you mean?" I ask, trying to keep my tone rigid, but it still saddens me to hear this.

"I went on my usual jog, but this time, I had no plans to go back to my apartment. I got to a bridge hundreds of feet above the river. I jumped over the little fence and stood there looking down into the water. I have no idea how long I stood there because time didn't mean anything to me anymore, and then I heard this voice close behind me."

"Who was it?" I wonder.

"Your mom."

I turn my head and look him in the eyes. That was a complete shocker. "No!"

"Your mom and I didn't meet the second time at a birthday party in Atlanta like we've told you over the years. We met at that bridge. She just so happened to be walking by." He looks to the side with a traumatized expression I have never seen on him before. "She talked me out of it."

I have never seen a single teardrop come out of my dad's eyes, let alone in public, but his eyes are red. Sadness flows down his cheeks. If I had been asked before today about the chances of my dad crying, I would have said I was more likely to win the lottery.

"Look." He recollects himself. "I'm mad at myself because I know how dangerous the mind can be, and, without a support system, it's almost impossible to not only live a happy life but want to live at all. And here I am, the man who promised when you were born to be there for you, help you, and talk to you about anything—and I now know I could have lost you."

***

On our way back home, it is a quiet ride, but my thoughts never stop.

Why can't parents be vulnerable? I don't get it! They always think they have to be perfect and great. Show some vulnerability! As a society, we would be so much better off, and relationships would really improve.

Although I am still hurt by his previous decision to hide such an important part of his past from me, I am relieved, and a lot of the tension and anger I held in my body is now gone. To have seen my father this way makes me believe he means what he is saying.

***

Later that day, I wrote in my journal.

From the beginning of time, physical health has been perceived to be the most important thing to us humans. If we can't use an arm or leg, our existence can potentially be compromised. We have needed our extremities for many vital actions. But for the longest time, we never paid attention to the mastermind that directs our extremities, actions, decisions, and most importantly, well-being—the brain. Our mental health is most important to us, but we don't prioritize it enough.

Unfortunately, whenever mental health is brought up, people think of weakness, softness, and vulnerability. You're not tough. I think men particularly have a harder time talking about their feelings and mental well-being because of the stereotypes associated with manliness.

After talking to my dad, I understand him better, and I know where he is coming from. He has certainly made a lot of progress from how his father was, but when it's my turn to be a father, I need to take it to the next step. I have to talk about mental issues.

My generation is making great strides to normalize the need to talk about mental health. Counseling is no longer perceived as the place where only crazy people go.

One thing I've realized from this whole situation is how unfair I was to my father by putting him on this pedestal. To me, he was the perfect person and father. I've felt bad for friends of mine for not having a father like mine. My mistake was thinking my dad was perfect when, in truth, nobody is. We all have our faults, and, in his case, he didn't want to show me his. That's the problem. We are conditioned to never show our less-than-perfect selves, our vulnerabilities.

I recognize that my dad has worked extremely hard for me to be where I am. Nothing in my life would be possible without my parents. They made sure I received the best medical attention and that I saw psychologists as soon as possible.

My dad called off of work for a couple of weeks, just to be close to me, even though I didn't speak to him. And if that isn't the perfect act of love from an imperfect father, then I don't know what is.

CHAPTER 6

A couple of years have passed, and I am now fourteen years old. Yesterday was a big day for both of us, and I find myself needing to express my thoughts in my journal. My dad and I have been invited to give a speech at the Dream Big Conference in Barcelona.

Yesterday was the first day of the event, and I thought it was pretty funny that everyone's name seemed to be "dreamer."

"Hey, Dreamer, how are you doing today?" says one person to me.

"You're up next, Dreamer?" another guy asks one of the presenters.

"Nice suit, Dreamer!"

What would you like to eat, Dreamer?"

And so on.

I heard the word dreamer so much yesterday that I was caught off guard when someone said my actual name back at the hotel.

The theme of this event is to bring dreamers together and talk about the dreams we have. Some of them are just thoughts, while others are being worked on or are already complete. It's basically an innovation hub with potential investors determining who to throw their money at.

The coolest dream I have heard so far is by this guy named Paco. His idea is to create a food tunnel system that connects all kitchens from houses and restaurants, and people at home can order what they want online, and it will literally come right to their kitchen. I love food, and if this ever exists in my lifetime, I will be the happiest person on Earth.

In general, though, the beauty of dreams is that they have no boundaries. When people limit their dream, they also limit their potential, which limits the worth of their existence. We are dreamers by nature, but we repress them to appear mature.

***

I wake up to day two of the event, my dad's, and my day to present. It was hard to sleep last night with all the nervousness really starting to control my body. It made me feel like I had to pee every other moment, but in reality, I didn't. At this point, my insides should be as dry as a desert. My jokes too.

I'm in the kitchen eating a granola bar just to get something in my system when my dad comes looking for me.

"Hey, Marco, you ready to go?" he asks, clearly ready to leave.

I'm not, but the show must go on. "Yeah, sure. Just let me go to the bathroom real quick, and then I'll meet you at the car."

"Okay," he agrees, seeming pleased that I'm ready without needing any further convincing.

I pack up the rest of my granola bar and head to the bathroom for hopefully the last time.

As I make my way out, I can hear my brother and sister talking at the entrance.

"I would be so nervous if I had to talk in front of a lot of people," my brother admits.

"I would be too," she replies without any hesitation.

Well, that's not helping, but they're twelve and ten anyway. What do they know?

"Let's go!" My dad elevates his voice toward my siblings. "Mom is already in the car."

He always likes to be at places super early. If he had a national flight at 10:00 a.m., he'd be there at 7:00 a.m. at the latest. Just in case the impossible happens, and they decide to switch *airports* instead of gates.

***

We get to the underground private parking area in the back of a wide and long building.

This venue is also where they have the Mobile World Congress Conference, with over one hundred thousand visitors every year. The venue is called Fira de Barcelona, and it is about fifteen minutes from the hotel and five minutes from the port.

We all pile out of the car and hurry inside. Some of the higher members of the conference, with their beautifully clean and shiny suits, see us come in and introduce themselves. I'm just wearing a short-sleeved shirt and some jeans. If there is a dress code, I certainly didn't get it. My dad is a little better off with a long-sleeved shirt and some regular pants.

While everyone is smiling, I'm dying a little bit inside, and I just want to run home and hide under my bed. I have that awful sensation where my mouth feels really tight and dry. This feeling is the worst, almost like a fish out of water.

We are early, but my dad and I split off from my mom and siblings, and we head backstage and talk to some of the people. I see another kid who looks around my age, which is comforting, but in general, there are people of all ages, even ancient people. Hey, you are never too old to stop dreaming.

We get a little moment to ourselves, and I am trying to distract myself. I can't help but have this sense of overwhelming gratitude that my dad is here. Overall, our relationship is back to what it was before my hospitalization a few years ago. Actually, it is better than it was because I don't have to hide anything, and he doesn't feel like he needs to either. I still go to therapy, and I don't have to take the meds as frequently as I used to.

"Do you think we could go see an NBA game when we go to LA next week?" I ask my dad. We are heading there to pitch our new idea, which we are giving a generic overview for at our conference presentation today.

"Do you know if they have a home game?"

"I don't know. I didn't check."

"I'll look later, but if they do, then certainly yes."

Seeing Kobe play would be amazing.

***

We're just a few moments away from showtime, and my dad smiles at me with confidence and calmness. I try to replicate that, but I don't think it's working.

"Ladies and gentlemen, please welcome Tomas and Marco as they discuss the beginning of the global classroom," the speaker announces, welcoming us to the stage.

As we are walking on, I can hear large applause. I can even hear younger voices screaming. I wonder if any of my classmates are here. That would be amazing!

My dad and I get into place, and he begins.

"A couple of years ago, our website started as a simple idea to connect students, schools, the internet, and social media. We did our research, we handed out surveys, we conducted many interviews, and eventually, we concluded that it was worth giving a shot."

Wow, every time he says that I get happy flashbacks to those days. It feels like forever ago.

"After a few months of trying to figure out how to get it built, we finally did, and a little over two years ago, on February 14, 2010, we published the site."

The crowd applauds, and I start clapping too until I remember I am also one of the presenters. I need to get it together.

He looks at me, smiling, before continuing, "Since then, it has grown tremendously and beyond anything Marco and I—and anyone else on the team—could have ever imagined. A big part of that was the early and amazing support from students, parents, schools, public and private organizations, and even some governments."

I know my dad has only one more line left before it is my turn to speak. I freeze. *What is my part?*

Got it!

"Most importantly, independent research has demonstrated that students around the world are benefiting from our platform, both in an academic sense and from the pleasure perspective of sharing their journey in school with others."

My dad slowly looks over at me, and a few people scream out of excitement. Here I go.

"To all of the eleven-year-olds out there, and if you are not eleven, then think back to those times if you can still remember them."

People in the crowd laugh.

I laugh a little with them and press on, "At that age, basically no one has a shortage of dreams. Essentially, everything is a dream because we haven't had much time to do anything yet. We tell our parents what we want to become... firefighters, astronauts, basketball players, or whatever other cool thing we can think of. And often, those that don't stop dreaming can achieve those amazing things."

I pause and take a sip of water from the bottle I brought onstage. I see comedians do that all the time, so I might as well do that too. I am feeling good now.

"It soon became apparent to us that this is bigger than we originally thought. I am not talking about the website, though, I am talking about the future of education. This is where one big dream leads to another big dream because we never stopped dreaming. Remember, there are no boundaries to dreams. Reality only kicks those who want an excuse to not entertain their dreams."

Before I can say my next line, the audience bursts into applause, and I can't help but grin. My dad looks over to me with a proud expression, and after the noise dies down a bit, he encouragingly nods at me to keep going.

"What the classroom looks like now, which is basically a network of silos, will eventually become an interconnected ecosystem benefiting all stakeholders."

This is becoming fun. I am getting the hang of it.

"Before we get into that, I want to first give you a little bit more backstory on our journey. By the time that first summer came around, about four months after we launched, we reached out to local schools and county school system directors, trying to see if we could collaborate with them on making our platform better by finding out what their needs, requirements, and challenges were."

With this, I figuratively pass the mic back to my dad, and he confidently steps back in. "This began solely as a small-scale outreach program to learn more about what schools are doing, what they are working on, how much technology and software they use, and their vision for moving forward. As you can imagine"—my dad smiles—"some schools weren't interested in talking to us because they didn't take us seriously."

Yeah, we got a lot of rejections. I nod in agreement. And I mean a lot! But from the few that spoke to us, we learned so much. We owe them big time.

"By the following summer, we didn't have to do much outreach because we were bombarded with emails and calls from principals, directors, headmasters, and presidents of schools at all levels from all around the world. We had to quickly expand our teams and divide the work into continents and sometimes even countries because it was a lot. We hired people with knowledge in that respective geographical zone and put them in charge of that segment."

He looks to me, confirming it's my turn again.

"On a personal level, it has been amazing to learn about all the different ideas and teaching methods and tools from schools everywhere in the world—those they use and have requested us to implement.

"And as we learned more about the schools, we started generating this concept of the 'school of tomorrow.' The 'I go to school at such and such' we believe will no longer exist. We are not there yet because we still have a vast number of students around the world who don't even have access to a traditional education, let alone technology devices."

"That's exactly right, Marco," my dad says on cue. "And we believe there will be a universal schooling model that is neither fully remote nor fully in person. A hybrid student experience. Students will be able to take classes from anywhere, including in person. You could take an algebra class in Saudi Arabia, Argentina, or Italy. Everyone is under the same rigorous curriculum, which means everyone's diploma or grades are worth the same. This is one of the biggest issues in today's world. Why is the worth of a diploma in country x worth more than in country y, even though the curriculum in country y is tougher than in country x?

"We believe this system will be much more cost-effective than the traditional model because of the economies of scale. The purpose isn't to create profit. Instead, the sole mission is to educate students around the world as flexibly and inclusively as possible to provide every student with opportunities to succeed. Such a system would highly benefit governments because it would reduce costs significantly."

"That's exactly right, Dad," I say in my most over-the-top grown-up voice, mimicking his exact words from only a moment before.

As I hoped for, a deep chuckle ripples through the audience, and my dad laughs along too. After a moment, I take the quieting noise as my sign to continue.

"Traditional high school paths limit the potential of many students throughout the world. They take classes they will never again in their lives need, and they will forget most of what they learned throughout their educational years."

"Exactly!" someone shouts from the audience, followed by a sea of nodding heads, all knowing the dilemma I'm talking about.

"The curriculum of tomorrow is a highly flexible and student-centered program that will prepare students who are leaving high school to be way more organized and advanced than they are today. The model is flexible in the sense that it caters toward the path of the student. Unlike in college, where many students can only have one major due to time and monetary reasons, this program will have many small specializations from kindergarten through twelfth grade that will allow students to gain certifications for completing those tracks.

"We envision a core set of classes, but this core is greatly reduced from the plethora of core classes most schools offer around the world today. Every student must then complete either six small specializations, three major specializations, or one super-major specialization for those who know for sure what they want to do.

"It's important that kids have plenty of opportunities to figure out what they want to end up doing, which is why no student is forced to continue on a track they first select. We often don't end up finding what we want to do until many years after school. Instead of wasting valuable years by making them go through a system that leaves them clue-less, the curriculum of tomorrow will have them graduate in great shape."

My dad takes a small step forward, signifying that it is his turn but pauses long enough to allow my message to sink in.

"Before we end, I want you all to imagine how field trips would work. For example, an organizer here in Barcelona sets up field trips for students in the area. Students can then decide to join it or not, and they can continuously meet new people, take part in great experiences, and, all the while, find even more that interests them.

"We will leave you with this, my fellow dreamers. Just dream. Dream about how you see the world and put it to action. At the end of the day, dreams shape our future, so don't let everyday life shape yours. Thank you!"

As if we planned it, the whole crowd jumps to their feet and erupts in the loudest applause I have ever heard. For a moment, I am absolutely stunned, but within seconds, I am grinning from ear to ear.

Wow, what a relief. My dad and I smile at each other and even embrace, still onstage. A few waves to the crowd, and off we go.

I didn't even realize how much I was sweating until my mom pointed it out. What can I say? I had a great time!

CHAPTER 7

—

It's Tuesday morning, about six months after the conference. I'm in Lagos, Nigeria, to visit some of the head educators in the city and country and take a trip to the fishing town of Makoko. This informal settlement happens to be one of the poorest and most vibrant slums in Nigeria. About one hundred thousand people live on stilts on the lagoon, which is why some people call it the "Venice of Africa."

These last few months, I have been traveling the world and meeting many educational leaders, teachers, and students— not only to see how we can improve the website and get more feedback on our "education of the future" idea but also as a part of my journey to learn more about different cultures. Of course, I should be trying to learn and figure myself out first, but that's boring.

What is interesting is how many of these places are so similar yet so different at the same time.

***

I met my new friend, Samuel, at the conference. He is my age. We got permission from his family, and he is letting me stay at their home for this next week while I meet with the educational leaders. My dad met Samuel's family at the conference and is confident I'll be in good hands while I'm here. Samuel presented by himself at the event and is nothing short of a genius, so if his family is anything like him, I know my dad is absolutely right.

His family lives in a beautiful house in the neighborhood of Ikeja that looks to be well off. With high ceilings and many different colors inside and outside the house, everything feels incredibly spacious and nothing short of luxurious.

His family agreed to show me around the city while I'm here, and from what I have seen so far, Ikeja has a huge mall, many restaurants, hotels, and a country club, so I'm looking forward to getting started.

After we eat some amazing jollof rice with vegetables and beef, Samuel's cousin, Richard, is now taking us to meet with some of the local chiefs, teachers, and students in Makoko. Chief Simbeye will give us a little tour of the town and take us to the floating school in the area. Not too long ago, I remember seeing the floating school online, with three floors made by a local architect here in Lagos, and I was completely amazed. I had never seen that before, which is a brilliant idea, especially considering so many people here live on the water.

Now that I am really starting to make money with this business, I definitely want to start donating a portion of the profits, and this could be the starting place.

As we are getting closer to our destination, I can see many high-rises in Lagos Island, on the other side of the river. From what Samuel told me, that is the main business district in Lagos. I wonder what types of companies are in those buildings because I'm not familiar with the Nigerian business landscape yet.

Meanwhile, Richard's voice changes to a state of shock, and since he is speaking in one of the local languages, I have no idea what he is saying. Either way, his tone tells me it is not good.

I look back out the window and decide to mind my business. The sky is beautifully blue today.

***

Nearly ten minutes later, Richard gets off the phone and tells us hundreds of girls were kidnapped at a secondary school in the northeast part of the country.

"What?" I exclaim.

"Yes, during the night and early this morning."

"Only girls?" I question, trying to make sense of this.

"Yes, it's an all-girls school."

Two hundred girls taken? I can't even imagine that happening in Europe or in the US. Those poor girls.

"Who did this?" I finally ask, still completely perplexed.

"Boko Haram."

I've never heard of them, and I wonder who they are.

As if reading my mind, Richard continues, "They are an Islamic militant group like Al-Qaeda and the Taliban, and they are located in northeast Nigeria."

I had no idea Nigeria had a militant group in the country. "How long have they been around?"

"We've been fighting them for years, but the situation has been getting worse and worse lately," he laments.

"Do you know any of the girls who were taken?"

"Yes, the sister of a church friend of mine is one of the girls. He is the one I just spoke to."

"Oh, no. Hopefully, they get them all out soon."

He nods in agreement, and with that, the car falls silent again, none of us knowing what to say next.

***

About twenty minutes later, we arrive at the outskirts of the Adogbo Village. This is one of six villages in Makoko and one of the four floating villages. An elderly man in elegant clothing stands only a few feet away from our parked car.

"Chief Simbeye?" I ask.

"It is," Samuel confirms.

I get out of the car with Samuel and Richard.

The chief first approaches Samuel's parents. They seem to know each other based on the extensive words they share. And then he approaches me. "Marco, we are so pleased to have you here."

"Thank you, Chief, for having me. Very kind of you."

The four of us wave goodbye to Samuel's parents, who will be picking us up later in the day.

"Well, before I get into the education aspect of our community, I first would like to give you a tour and introduce you to some notable people in the area. If that is okay with you, Marco?" He bows his head slightly.

"Absolutely, Chief! I would love a tour."

The chief guides Samuel, Richard, and me onto one of the many kayaks in the water.

"How big is Makoko, Chief?" I'm still thinking about the horrific kidnapping that took place, but I'm trying my best to be in this moment.

"It is very big, Marco. Some people estimate up to three hundred thousand people live here."

"Wow, that's bigger than a lot of cities I have been to."

"Well, Marco, as you can imagine, Makoko wasn't always like this. It started off as a small fishing town many centuries ago, and it has grown much since."

I see a kayak with a little kid guiding it, towing another one full with food to sell.

"What is the biggest challenge for the villages right now?" I am getting a lot of stares from other people in their kayaks and from their huts sustained by sticks above the water. They're probably wondering what I am doing here.

"The biggest challenge right now is definitely the government, and it has been that way for a long time."

"I'm guessing they are not the biggest fan of Makoko?"

"Basically, yes. Everyone who comes to Lagos, nationally or internationally, sees Makoko from our city's main bridge over there, and the government does not like that," he explains, pointing to the bridge in the distance and subtly shaking his head.

When we came over here, we crossed that bridge, and I did see Makoko. "What has the government done so far?"

"As far as help? Nothing. But as far as getting us out of here, they did try that several years ago. The State Ministry of Waterfront Infrastructure Development issued a seventy-two-hour quit notice to residents. Four days later, a bunch of men with machetes started breaking down buildings. The sad part is that one of the residents died from that encounter with the officials. With support from activists, we forced the government to stop their efforts to destroy this city, but they are still our biggest fear today. You never know what they could do next."

I nod, taking this in and looking around at the surrounding village. I'm surprised at how some of these huts are even standing. The whole structure of each one of them depends on wooden sticks that don't seem that strong to me. Imagine falling into the water at night while you're sleeping? Oh, no.

"How long have you been chief?" I ask.

"Since my father passed away twenty-three years ago." He laughs. "It has been a long time, and I know that because the Makoko fish market was fairly small back then, but now, people from all over the city come and buy our fish. It's cheaper than everywhere else, and it is still great quality."

As he mentions this, we get to the floating school. It looks even cooler in person than it does in the pictures. The first "floor" is one large, square-shaped, and big open space. The second floor is an even narrower square, and the third floor even smaller, creating a pyramid shape.

Four or so compartmentalized classrooms are on the second floor and one on the third. I am so astounded by the architecture. "This is amazing, Chief."

"Thank you! Our local architect did a great job, and he is going to make some more soon."

"Please let me know how I can help," I offer, already thinking of ways I could get involved.

"Thank you, Marco," he says, smiling at me. "That is kind of you to offer, and I will make sure to keep that in mind."

***

Later that day, I was so inspired by my experience from earlier that I knew exactly what my next journal entry would be.

We live in a world with finite resources. However, for billions of people, their resources are so restricted that life's basic necessities, such as nourishment and survival, require creativity and resilience to achieve.

Safety is not guaranteed, and unfortunately, in our world, it is a privilege and not a right to live a harmless life. The girls in Nigeria did not deserve to be kidnapped. They were merely students wanting to improve themselves and their country.

Makoko is a slum hustling and bustling to get people in better positions in life. Before we left, I was actually able to speak with the architect who grew up in Makoko. These days, he is world-renowned and creating problem-solving solutions, such as the one in this water city.

Resources might be finite, but it is what you do with them that counts.

CHAPTER 8

——

Several months later, it is the time of year most people absolutely love, Christmas. This year, my parents decided to take my brother and me to Indonesia for the first time. My sister really wanted to go visit some family and friends in Barcelona, so my parents let her do that instead.

Our hotel is right in front of the beautiful beach, and the water is as clear as what we have in our drinking bottles. After eating breakfast, the four of us head to the beach to swim for a little bit, which is nice and calm.

"The ocean looks farther out today than it was yesterday," my mom says.

It can be shallow on any given day—as we have experienced during many occasions, whether in Barcelona or Miami—but not to this degree and speed.

"Yeah, let's not go too far out," my dad agrees. "Remember when we got stuck out there in Greece?" He laughs while looking at my mom.

Must have been before my time.

"That was horrible! Never again." My mom shakes her head.

The story goes that my mom was in the ocean when a strong undercurrent suddenly pulled her out. My dad shouted advice and calming words from the shoreline. Eventually, she was able to get out.

As we start wading, the current seems to keep pulling farther and farther away.

I look back toward the shore, and we are already far out.

"I don't think this is a good idea," I say, even though I think it is cool that we are so far out, and it only reaches our waists. Normally, the water would be so deep, my brother would be underwater.

"What's happening?" My brother looks skeptically into the distance.

"Let's go back to the beach because that doesn't look right," my mom emphasizes.

As we start wading back, the lifeguards whistle for everyone to get out of the water immediately. All of us scramble through the water to safety as the breaking waves become shallower by the second. This must be more serious than we originally thought.

We get to the beach, but my dad yells at us from behind.

"Keep running!"

So we run past our belongings and onto the street. I don't know what he saw, but I don't question him. My brother and I are in front, and my parents are behind.

A lot of movement and nervousness is going on from people around us, and when I eventually do look back, my parents are nowhere in sight.

"James," I order, "Stick with me! I don't know where Mom and Dad are."

"Okay!" he shouts over the noise of abrupt wind and people screaming around us. He peers over my shoulder, hoping to see Mom and Dad in the distance, and I see the fear register in his eyes when he sees for himself that they're not.

A rush of water and debris hits me hard from behind. I manage to hold on to something solid from the building to my left.

"Grab my arm, James!"

I have him with my right hand, but it's hard for me to pull him close enough to the building so he can grab ahold of a support as well.

A lot more water pounds us, tugging him out of my grasp. "Hold me, Marco!" he cries, and I'm trying my best, but I'm losing my grip on him.

"Grab my arm instead of my hand!" I desperately tell him.

A metal piece hits him, and I am forced to watch as he disappears into chaos. *Where is he?*

I manage to climb up on the top of a small house as the current rises quickly. I look around, and I can't find my brother or my parents.

***

Several hours later, all of the water is gone, and I'm walking around, absolutely stunned by the mess the storm left behind. I want to help anyone who needs it, and I'm hopeful my family is close by, doing the same thing. I can't think any other way.

I call their names, but I see someone who looks hurt, and I rush to them. I am sickened with dread when I realize it's too late. They're already dead. That's when I notice... there are dead bodies everywhere. I fall to my knees at the loss of so many lives. People scream in pain, and adults carry dead children.

This can't be real. No way. Just hours ago, people were living in paradise.

***

Two days later, I still haven't found my family. I am volunteering at one of the campsites that have been set up. They have bulletin boards with people's names.

"Marco, come here, please." The leader of this camp is a doctor from Morocco who was also here on vacation.

"Coming." I run to her, ready to do the next task.

"We found your parents." She smiles at me.

Oh my God, that is amazing! I start crying out of happiness.

"They're at a hospital close by."

"Can I go see them?" I sob, wiping the tears off my face. I can't let my family see I was crying. I want to prove to them I stayed strong.

"Yes, Hisra is going to take you over there now."

"Thank you!" Finally, they found them. I go to turn to find Hisra, but she stops me with a gentle hand.

"We also found your brother…" She looks at me sadly and gives me a hug.

I can't feel my legs. I fall, but the doctor catches me. James was more than a brother. He was everything. Even with all the fame I got because of the website, he was my biggest supporter. He was always there with me. We did everything together. We hung out at school and played soccer and tennis. We would get at each other's throats playing Ping-Pong with remote controls as the net in between us, or we would go to the playground five minutes from home. My brother has been my constant X factor, with me everywhere.

He was running right in front of me. Now he is running right above me.

I feel a hand on my shoulder. It's the doctor's hand. She pulls me to her chest while I cry.

"Go to your parents, Marco. They really want to see you."

"Okay," I choke out, wanting nothing more than to be with them too.

I get up, and Hisra holds my hand for the whole walk, which feels like the longest walk I have ever had. The entire time, I think of running alongside James, of how confident I was that we were going to be okay. Then, in a matter of seconds, everything changed.

∗∗∗

We finally get to a building with more people than space. Even from a few hundred feet away, a horrible, disgusting smell makes me want to throw up. I follow Hisra into the building and see people everywhere lying on the floor.

She stops. I look at her, and then I look forward. It's my parents. I spot them, but they haven't seen me yet. They look like they're in pain. A lot of pain. My mom is lying on a hospital bed with rusty legs, and my dad is sitting against the wall next to the bed with a pale face.

I slowly walk up to them, and my mom turns her head in my direction.

"Marco," my mom says, forcing a smile. Her eyes are red. I'm guessing they already know about James.

"What happened to you two? I looked back, and I didn't see you anymore. I just kept running forward with James, but…"

"We are okay, Marco," my dad tries to say in a calm voice.

A couple of days ago, they both looked like young people in their late forties with the excitement that comes from a happy time together, especially since we haven't had much quality family time lately. They now look like they have both aged twenty years.

"Are they okay?" I whisper at Hisra to make sure.

"Yes, they will be fine. Later today, they will be transported to the capital and then to France for treatment. You'll be going too."

My dad has bandages that cover his left eye and his right hamstring. My mom has bandages on her ankles, and I can't see her left hand. Scratches cover their bodies.

"And my broth—?" I can't even finish the word.

"We'll be sending him to France too."

"Thank you, Hisra."

"You're welcome. I have to head back, but someone will come here once it is time to go." I give her a big hug, and she hugs me back. "I wish you the best, Marco," she tells me and then leaves.

***

A month later, both of my parents are doing well again. Some minor injuries still, but overall, they are much better than they were in that hospital in Indonesia.

I have been going to a therapist ever since we came back.

"Any nightmares?" my therapist asks me, as she does every time we meet.

"Yes." I close my eyes. *Every night.* Literally every night, I have a bad dream about that day. "I was on the roof looking at the street to my right, and I could see a little girl walking innocently. Not crying or yelling or doing anything. Just walking around. She had a few cuts on her arms, but nothing major. I yelled to get her attention, and she eventually looked at me. I waved at her to come over, and she followed my directions. Right as she got close to me, another wave hit her before I could reach her." I pause. "And then I woke up. My pajamas were wet. My pillow and sheets were wet. My face and arms were wet. Everything was wet."

"Who did you see in that girl?"

Tears stream down my cheeks. My body shakes. "I saw... I saw my brother. I saw how a metal piece popped out of nowhere and knocked him out of my grip." I wasn't strong enough to hold him. I almost did, but at the last moment, I lost him. "His body rapidly turned, and the last thing I saw of him was his face." He was still conscious but crying hard. "Our eyes connected for a split moment, and I think we both realized it was the last time we would see each other." He tried all he could to grab onto my arm as we were losing hold of each other. "In the last moments, he kept swinging his arms at me like a dog absolutely needing to be held by his master."

I looked and looked and looked. I never saw his body above water again.

"His face is in my head all the time. That face of a younger sibling looking at the older sibling for help, but in this case, it was help to stay alive. And here I am, the older sibling, alive. And he is dead."

I can't live with that.

She doesn't reply immediately. It feels like an eternity, but I guess she wants me to have a moment to let it out.

"What you and your family went through, Marco, is horrible and sad. To open myself up to you a little bit, too—as a child, I witnessed domestic violence for some years until one day, my father killed my mother. I'm not saying this to make it about me. I just want you to know I felt a similar pain and anger, and I'm committed to helping you on this journey toward acceptance. It won't be a quick one, but if we do it right, you will be able to keep your brother in your heart while living a successful and enjoyable life."

You're blind to some pain until you go through it. I never thought my brother could cause me so much pain. The most he had ever inflicted on me was accidentally kicking a soccer ball into my private parts. That was painful, but it went away. This pain will never go away.

Who am I supposed to yell at now? Who am I supposed to fight with? Who am I supposed to snitch on? Who am I supposed to steal candy from? Who am I supposed to do all these terrible things to? All these terrible things—along with so many more positive things—make you love someone so much without even knowing it. I will never live an enjoyable life without him.

"Cool," I say anyway.

***

Three months later, my parents, sister, and I are sitting in a plane heading back to Indonesia. Even though my sister wasn't there with us, she seems to be the most shocked about what happened. Maybe she feels guilty that she was lucky enough not to be there with us. After a couple of days of not hearing from us, she got a bad feeling that something had happened to us, and her friend's parents confirmed it when they saw the tsunami on the news. It was a horrible realization for all of them when they recognized the disaster site was where we were staying. Even though they let her stay longer than planned with open arms, they all quietly knew things would never be the same.

We don't speak the entire way on the flight, which is something I have never done before. I feel this massive amount of tension on my shoulders from knowing where we are heading, but it's time. Time to go back and make sense of what happened.

Seeing all of the people helping each other and everyone doing their best helped me find my peace. Many of us suffered that day and will continue to suffer for the rest of our lives, but we all have this bond together. We have each other, and we promised to never forget that.

We are one.

CHAPTER 9

———

I have been writing more lately as a form of meditation.

It has been five years since I lost my brother in Indonesia, and recently, I lost a good friend who I considered my second brother. Even being twenty years old, it's still a hard loss to take.

Since Indonesia, a lot has changed. When I was sixteen, we moved to the United States, and after getting there, I requested my role in the company to be reduced to that of a consultant when needed.

I went back to an in-person school setting, something I had not been in since the "overnight" success when I was eleven.

Today, I will write from my desk about race, racism, and my close friend, John, who passed away earlier in the week.

***

Until we moved to the States, I didn't understand there was a difference between black people and white people. My dad is black and my mom is white, and I didn't even realize they "belong" to completely different racial groups until I came here. I had been oblivious for sixteen years, not because racism doesn't exist in Europe or the other places I have lived, but because it was never spoken about in my surroundings. Here, talks about race are front and center in so many conversations.

For example, as a new kid in eleventh grade, I strongly remember every single day at school hearing a person calling another student either "white boy," the N-word, or other ways of addressing people based on race. I realized these words, although completely new to me, were often another way of saying *bro*.

I had never once thought about my family's or my own skin color. Did I know we have different skin colors? Yes, of course, I did. I am not colorblind, but seeing the difference doesn't mean you understand it.

***

John and I graduated from high school in June 2017, and I decided to move onto Barry University's campus. Fortunately, that was only twenty-five minutes away from our neighborhood, so we still hung out once in a while. He would sometimes come to campus, and we would go watch the basketball team play. During our senior year in high school, he tried out and made Barry's team, but they weren't offering him enough scholarship money for him to attend the school.

We didn't see each other for almost my whole second semester because I got busy with classes, and I was also distracted by college life.

Toward the end of the semester, I got a call from a local number I hadn't seen before, but I picked up anyway just in case it was something important. A whispering, panicking voice on the other end sounded like John holding back tears.

Just to make sure it was him, I called his name. "John?"

"Marrrrrrco," he managed to get out. I could tell he was literally losing it.

"John, what's going on?" I demanded.

"I'm in jail!" His voice cracked when he said *jail*.

My heart dropped. No way on Earth would I think he would be in jail, not even for a split second. He would never do anything to get himself there.

After what felt like forever, I asked him a couple of questions, feeling like my own voice was going to crack. "I'll come over now."

He collected himself. "No, just let my mom know my bail hearing is tomorrow. If they let me out on bail, can you have them pick me up?"

"Of course! I will tell your mom now."

"Thanks, Marco. One of the officers is waving at me to come."

"Everything will be alright," I reassured him.

He hung up the phone.

Little did I know that everything was not going to be alright. What was supposed to be a fifteen-year sentence for something he did not do ended up becoming a death sentence.

***

The last time I saw John was the day before he died. This was my first week back home from college and with no school stuff on my mind. A few Mondays away from starting my first internship, I didn't want to think about any of that. Instead, I was determined to visit John as much as the correctional center would let me.

I arrived at the facility on Monday and went through the standard process for visitors. It's never quick, but finally, I was able to walk in through the last door to get to the visitation room, where I saw him seated on the other side of the glass at the station all the way to the left.

At this point, I always told myself to forget my problems and be the best friend I could be. I wanted to make him hopeful and excited about life after prison. His face immediately told me that this past month had been horrible. He was looking less and less like that happy, cool guy everybody knew in high school. He even has a few cuts around his left eye. John never got into fights.

He didn't say hi, and he didn't have his usual smile. He looked mad, tired, and despairing all at the same time. He sat down with his hands covering his face, and after thirty seconds of sitting there, he opened his mouth.

"Man, I don't know how much longer I can last!" he burst out.

I guess this will be a serious conversation. "You already know I think you will be walking out of here soon."

John shook his head hard. "I don't know, Marco. I've only been in here for a year, and I just can't anymore." He added in a whispering but panicky voice, "I feel like one of these bitches is going to kill me."

John never cussed unless he was excited in a good way, and so to hear him cussing then worried me because that was not him.

I was not going to address the killing part, so I whispered back, "How are the correctional officers?"

"It's a lottery," John said without whispering back. "One day, you get the good officer who doesn't abuse his power to satisfy his ego. Then, the next day, you have his opposite who will beat the living crap out of you for no reason."

"Is that what happened to your face?" I blurted without thinking. I had been trying not to stare at his left side since we sat down, but it had to be mentioned at some point.

"No, that was an inmate," he told me with a look that said I shouldn't ask further.

The same inmate who damaged his face also killed him.

***

Like me, John had big dreams. First, it was basketball, but then he decided to focus on entrepreneurship, as he was always the type of guy to come up with solutions to smaller and, in recent years before prison, bigger problems.

At last, I had someone who wasn't considerably older than me who could challenge my thoughts. He made me think of things I had never even thought about in my life, and his passion for environmental sustainability took shape with his young businesses.

He loved his community and family. Overtown, which was once called Colored Town during the Jim Crow era, was South Florida and Miami's historic commercial center in the black community. With the construction of highways right through the center of Overtown, the area became economically destitute and considered a ghetto. Businesses closed, and productivity stagnated in the neighborhood.

After high school graduation, John enrolled in the local community college at the Downtown branch of Miami Dade College, which made me a short bus ride away from him. With the grades he had in high school, he would pay nothing for his associate's degree.

One summer evening, while we were playing one-on-one basketball, he got a call from the hospital. His mom had gotten into a car accident on I-95, heading back home from work at Aventura Mall. A drunk driver ran right into the back of her car, causing her to lose control and veer into the wall to her right. For those who believe in God... I have seen pictures of that accident, and that was one special act of grace. And for those who believe in miracles... this was about the biggest miracle you could ever think of. She was lucky her gas tank did not explode. John's mom survived the car accident, but she had broken bones, dislocated parts, a lost eye, and poorly functioning organs. Not in the slightest an exaggeration. And for John who, again, comes from a low economic status in America... You guessed it right; hospital bills were through the roof.

His mom was basically paralyzed, and with the financial burden on John's shoulders to take care of his mom and younger siblings, he did what everybody—including John—didn't want him to do. He dropped out of college and focused solely on working and making money. Deep down, he knew he had no other option.

∗∗∗

Everything happened so fast, even thinking back now, I don't how things could have gone left so quickly and why they schemed against John the way they did.

The day he was arrested, he had asked to borrow a car from a white colleague from his work, where he had been working part-time for years already. John was heading to an interview for a full-time position, which would have paid him fairly well.

On his way there, he was stopped by the police. John had done nothing wrong, but they decided to look around the car. From the back window, they could see plastic containers, which appeared to contain some type of white powder. I was told later they were half open. It ended up being cocaine, and it was quite a significant amount.

The colleague denied it was his, the containers had been wiped clean of any fingerprints, and the rest is history.

***

A set of words has been floating around my head for a little while now as I reflect more on myself, my surroundings, and everything going on in the world.

First, I was just thinking about living in many different places and coming from a diverse background, but John's death has made me realize how these three words are bigger than I originally thought.

Here they are:

The foreign national.

CHAPTER 10

"Do a TED Talk," I have been told before.

My response has always been to grin. I was not against it, but at the same time, what would I possibly discuss? Would I talk about the company? My dad and I have done plenty of speeches on it already.

In the last year, though, I have been writing more than I have been speaking, and this process of putting words on paper makes me think about a lot of different things in the world. So, a couple months ago, when I was invited to give a speech at a TED Talk event in New York City, I was excited and immediately knew what I was going to talk about. I was going to speak on the topic of the foreign national, which is personal to me and, I believe, personal to many other people.

***

When I arrive at the Town Hall theater and walk onstage for the first time, I feel like Michael Phelps could swim laps on this stage; it's so big. The lights are blinding, and there is a lot of clapping at first, but as soon as I get ready to begin, utter silence takes over.

It's showtime.

"We live in a world divided by borders." My voice sounds like it's traveling into eternity. "Think about it. Every country"—I remind myself to use my hands to get comfortable—"has borders that neighbor other ones or the ocean. Within every country, we have states or regions separated by borders. Here in the US, within states we have counties, and within counties we have cities, and within cities and towns we have neighborhoods."

I'm trying to find faces to connect with, but I feel blind.

I walk a few steps over to the large notepad that has been set up for my speech and draw lines for the audience to see. "For all I know, your children could have drawn these lines better." I smile, and a little giggle comes from the crowd. "And obviously, there is more to the story on that end. Historians in the room could tell me all about how every line came into existence, but today I'm going to look at these lines figuratively."

I walk to the other side of the stage before pressing on.

"We are taught from a young age, whether intentionally or not, that everyone within a perimeter belongs to a country, a community of like-minded people, and more importantly, a big family."

I lift my arms in an imaginary hug for the people around me.

"Let me give you an example."

Shoot, what was the example? Ah, got it.

"If one of you goes to the Philippines twenty hours from here and you hear an American speak at a local market, you're reminded of home. Maybe"—I raise my eyebrows—"you might even smile and speak to the person. Or"—I point to the crowd—"you're in the Philippines to escape Americans, and you can't stand the fact that you would come across one so far away."

The crowd laughs.

"Well, regardless of how trivial the bond is, there still is one. In this case, because of the shared nationality. So back to these borders. I think many of us agree that they have been blurring in the last half century or so. You can fly to most places and stay there temporarily or even permanently. A good example is the European Union, which allows for free movement of the citizens of its member countries. So there's been change... somewhat."

I shrug.

"But strong belief systems about *us* and *them* still exist in many people's minds all around the world—based on numerous factors such as race and ethnicity."

This is the moment I would love to have a stool with a towel and a bottle of water like the stand-up comedians always have, so I could wipe my face and get a good sip of water.

"This belief governments like to put out that 'we, the people of a nation, are united under one flag, under one defined territory, under one government, and together as one population' sounds great, but unfortunately is rarely ever the case." I look around in disbelief.

"Is that true?" I ask the audience.

I hear a few *nos*.

"Of course not! Absolutely not! That could not be farther from reality. As long as we have people in high-ranking positions telling us these obvious lies, the longer it will take for us to come together."

I press my fist to my head and pull it away, springing my hand open as I do. *Mind blown.*

"You can't fix a problem if you don't identify it to begin with. Anyway, I'm a lucky SOB." I bow my head slightly and show the palms of my hands to the audience. "Excuse my French, I know you weren't ready for that."

I hear some laughter.

"But it's true."

The crowd is clearly amused.

"I was born in Atlanta, then we moved to London, then to Barcelona, then to Koblenz in Germany, then to Miami… you get the point."

I pause.

"I promise you I am not trying to rub it in." I grin. "I'm just trying to prove my point, you know? These are the places I grew up, and I often found myself asking, 'Who am I? What is my race, my nationality? What do I really enjoy doing?' Depression has been a big story of my life…"

I pause again, staring out at the silent crowd, letting them make the connection between not knowing where you belong and the effect on your mental health.

"When someone asks me where I am from, I either freeze or have all these questions in my head." I count them out with my fingers. "Which place should I say? Where I was born? Should I say somewhere else? Should I describe the whole story? I don't know. To some, these are trivial questions, but to others like me, these can easily become life-long questions."

I'm in my groove now.

"Everywhere I went, I was always told I was from somewhere else. When I was in Spain, I was the British kid. When I was in Germany, I was the Spaniard. In the States, I became the German guy."

I make a *what the heck* face.

"I never chose these nationalities; they were always assigned to me. I'll give you an example."

Somebody sneezes.

"Bless you. Um, train of thought, okay. It's eleventh grade, and we just moved to Miami. Kids I met asked me, 'Where you from?'

"In my mind, I was like, 'Let me tell you the full story.'

"And then the next day, a friend of one of those people told me, 'Oh, I heard you were from Germany.'

"I reply, 'Germany?'

"I was thinking, 'When did I say I was from Germany?'

"I told their friend all the places I had lived, and they picked the location I lived in the shortest time? What the heck?

"People don't like complex answers. They want to narrow it down so they can easily label you, whether they do it intentionally or not. So no matter how cool my story was to the people I met or how many places I had lived, I was doomed from the beginning to be represented by one of their choices."

I can see the crowd all nodding in one flowing wave. I think this talk is going well. My message is reaching them.

"I didn't like that. By assigning a specific nationality to me, they viewed me based on the stereotypes that come with it. I didn't want that. Thinking back, I guess my underlying hope was that my multiracial, multicultural background would mean people would see me for who I am rather than through their preconceived notions. All the different experiences have shaped me into who I am today. But my thinking did not stop with me because even though our full individual package is unique, we are made up of many shared features and experiences. Across the world, millions upon millions of people, if not billions, do not feel the sense of pride and comfort they wish or expect to have with their country of birth, residence, or attachment. So I ask myself, Why is this?"

I act like I'm thinking when I need a moment to breathe. I feel like I've been talking too long already.

"These people are not treated as first-class citizens because of the color of their skin, their religion, their immigration status, their gender, or any other distinction that makes one 'lesser' than the other in some people's eyes. The reasons why someone may not feel at home, even if they have never stepped outside their country, are limitless! For some, the level of detachment is greater than for others. I'm thinking of the people who are trapped in the endless cycle of oppression and poverty. I'm thinking of women and their struggle for equality in a patriarchal world. I think of the little kids working endless hours. I think of these people.

"I've seen a lot over the course of my twenty-one-year span, and some of you might know I was eleven years old when my dad and I started the website. My view of the world has changed a lot in the years between then and now. Then, I was so excited about the popularity, money, and fame from the website, but things quickly changed. It wasn't making me happy, and if anything, it was making things worse for me. I spent some time in the hospital for depression and questioned the meaning of my life. Even today, I still see a therapist.

"What I realized is that what I enjoy most is learning about different cultures and helping people. What we all share, despite our different backgrounds, is the foreign national experience. Foreign nationals exist within countries, states, and communities, and some of these people may have never stepped outside of their localities, but you do not have to be outside your country to feel foreign. Many people here in the United States feel just as foreign as the tourist who first arrived yesterday at the JFK airport.

"You only feel connected to a person, a group, or a nation if you are treated as every human being deserves to be treated. With respect, fairness, equal treatment, dignity, and so forth. As you already know, these values are nothing out of the norm. Just basic qualities we all expect from our neighbors. For example, a police officer questioned my mom because she was with my dad, who is black. I am certain that many black people here in America would consider themselves foreign nationals. Like that of my grandfather, their families have been in the United States for centuries, yet many of them still feel as though they are not a part of this country. They do not receive the same education or job opportunities as whites do. They suffer from police brutality, unlike anywhere else in the world.

"There is a wide network of foreign nationals out there, and it is time to recognize each other and unite for a better world."

CHAPTER 11

———

A week after the TED Talk, I am back in town for a few days. I am meeting up with my mom for a nice lunch at La Española. My dad is traveling back from work tonight, so I'll see him then. Now that I'm the legal drinking age, I could try out one of their signature Rioja wines, but I have never tried alcohol, and I don't plan on doing so soon.

I am waiting outside the restaurant, and I see my mom parking on the other side of the road. I wave to get her attention and smile when she sees me, excitedly waving back. I watch as she makes her way to the crossing light. She pauses until it turns green. I turn around and tell a passing waiter I would like a table for two.

Boom!

I snap my head back when I hear the bang. Something got hit hard, and the squeaking of a car's brakes is so high-pitched that my ears throb. I turn around to see a lady roll off the windshield of an Audi onto the ground about a hundred feet away. She's lying right in this massive intersection and bleeding badly. I look at the Audi, and the man panics and looks around. A second later, he speeds right past the lady and over one of her arms.

Stunned, I look over to see what my mom thinks. Should we go help that poor woman? But when I glance to the other side of the crosswalk, she's nowhere to be found. Where's my mom? Just a moment ago, I saw her waiting for the crossing light to turn green.

A chill races down my spine.

Wait a second... Is that...? No! It can't be! I rush to the lady, and as I get closer, I go faster.

It's my *mom*! What? Why?

I'm going to kill that son of a bitch!

Her body is facing mostly up. Her right arm is lying on the ground, stretched away from her body at the level of her face. The left arm, the one he ran over, looks completely fractured in several places with a zigzag form.

I turn my mom completely on her back. She's a mess, covered in blood and bruises. I start giving her CPR, inter-locking my fingers on top of her ribcage. Thirty compressions and two breaths. They taught me how to do this.

"Wake up, Mom," I whisper. "Wake up, please. I need you to wake up. Wake up!"

She is not waking up. Just a moment ago, I saw her smile, full of happiness. I need that back now! "Come on! I know you are going to wake up!"

I feel a light push on my shoulders, moving me out of the way. It's the ambulance EMTs.

"We got this, sir," one of them says to me, already taking over.

I nod reluctantly and move to the side.

For the first time in what feels like forever, I look up and see a whole bunch of people just watching.

No cars are moving. Everyone is stopped in all directions. I look back at my mom, and tears flood my cheeks. She looked so beautiful, as always, with her nice summer dress. But now, it is ripped with cuts with blood all over her. I crawl over to her, to wipe the blood from her face, but one of the EMTs holds me back.

"Please, let us do our job, sir!"

I fall to the side in a fetal position and cover my eyes.

She's dead. She's dead. She's *dead*!

Why?

Was that the last time I will ever see her alive?

I'm soaked in her blood, and one of the other EMTs approaches me to see if I am okay.

***

A couple of weeks later, I'm at the funeral with my father, sister, and other relatives.

It's my dad's moment to give the eulogy.

"And now I invite Ines's husband Tomas to share his thoughts," says the pastor.

My dad slowly walks up to the pulpit, sobbing.

I take my criticism back—nothing is worse than seeing someone who never cries show such vulnerability.

"Th-thank you for coming here today in remembrance of the life of my dear and beautiful wife, Ines," he stutters. "Twenty years ago, we met by chance. That is, at least, what many people would tell us. What is the probability that we would be on the same small island—Fiji—many thousands of miles away at the same time? I saw her at the beach while I was getting out of the water from my daily morning swim."

He smiles.

"Beautiful."

He pauses.

"I found some courage deep down inside and approached her with little hope of her even acknowledging me. I was ready to get turned down." He grins. "Little did I know that we would be spending a lot of time together for the remainder of our trip.

"Her flight was a couple of days before mine, and I remember the deep sadness I felt, not only because she was leaving but also because I didn't know if I would ever see her again. Fast-forward a couple of years, and after traveling to many other places, I was back in my hometown, Atlanta, but in a bad psychological place. I had been fighting depression for years, and I was ready to give up. To give you a little bit of perspective, this was around the 1996 Olympics in Atlanta. An event like that would normally bring me so much happiness, but it did not this time. One day I was standing on the edge of a bridge, looking down at the water hundreds of feet below me, ready to jump off."

My dad looks up into the audience with tear-filled eyes. "And then I heard a familiar female voice call my name. I did not even have to turn my head because I instantly knew who it was. Ines saved my life. Something..." He chuckles. "Something I obviously failed to do for her."

My dad tries to collect himself, but he is struggling.

"These last twenty years have been nothing short of a dream. We traveled the world and did so many cool things together. Some of those will never be shared with the outside world." He manages to laugh a little.

"She was the supporter I never had. She helped me get out of the deep hole I was in and made me realize I could enjoy life once more. She is the person I wanted to have a family with and spend the rest of my life with. She is everything to me and I will forever be indebted to her. I love you, Ines, and I miss you very... very much!"

That eulogy makes me tear up.

The pastor proceeds with the closing words as I try not to cry. "We have been remembering with love and gratitude a life that touched us all. I encourage you to help, support, and love those who grieve most. Allow them to cry, to hurt, to smile, and to remember. Grief works through our system in its own time. Remember to bless each day and live it to the full in honor of life itself—and to Ines. We often take life for granted, and yet it is the greatest gift God gave us."

Now to the blessings.

"'The Lord bless you and keep you; the Lord make his face shine on you and be gracious to you; the Lord turn his face toward you and give you peace.' So then, go in peace, and the God of all peace go with you. Amen."

Amen.

***

We are on our way back to the car from the cemetery, and I don't even know what to think about life anymore. The philosopher David Benatar argues that nonexistence is better than existence. In moments like these, I don't see why he would be wrong.

The pain you feel when you lose someone so important to you is immensely intense, and it makes you feel like life can't continue without that person.

I have only been to two funerals in my life, both for close family members—my mom and my brother. All I have left now are my father and my little sister.

"Don't ever leave me," I tell my dad.

"I will never leave, Marco."

"If you leave…"

My dad grabs me and gives me a big hug.

***

Even though I still have my dad, losing my mom made me want to visit orphanages to listen to the stories of children who never knew their parents or lost them at some point in their youth.

"Hi, Marco. We *are* grateful to have you, and thank you very much for coming," Tina, the director of The New Orphanage, greets me.

"Thanks for having me, Tina. This means a lot to me," I say, smiling out of excitement to be here.

"The kids will be so thrilled to see you!"

"Well, I can't wait to see them either. How old are they?" I lift and lower my hand above and below my shoulders, using height as a metaphor for age.

"All ages, Marco. We take in everybody. Even babies."

"That's nice of you—and everyone involved in making this happen." I smile at her. "What would you say is your biggest challenge right now?"

"Scaling, certainly. We need more capacity because the number of children people request us to take in is outpacing the amount of space we have, the number of programs our staff can run, and the budget we have to work with. So, unfortunately, we have been turning down a lot of kids, especially lately, because of the limitations we face."

"If I may ask, who helps with funding?"

Tina and I begin walking inside of the building.

"The majority of the money comes from fundraisers we organize every year, and we also get some money from the local and state governments."

"And how are those going?"

"It is getting better every year, which is, of course, amazing for us because we are also seeing new donors. But the scaling issue remains. Our increasing expenses are exceeding what we take in, and so that makes it hard to help as many children as we would like."

One of the kids approaches us. He has a Band-Aid on one of his eyes, and he looks a lot like my brother. He looks to be the same age.

"Hasan, this is Marco," Tina introduces us.

"Hi, Marco," Hasan says while distracted by a toy.

All of a sudden, I feel like I can't speak. So many memories are coming back, but I manage to reply, "Hi, Hasan."

Hasan smiles at me, holds Tina's leg for a little bit, and then runs away.

"His family sold him shortly after they arrived in the United States, but he managed to escape. He doesn't speak at all about it."

Behind every face, there is a story, and behind that story is a whole different world.

CHAPTER 12

———

It has been ten months since I lost my mom that tragic day, but life is so short, and I am too young to give up.

I have no better way to cheer up than to be in the house of one of the funniest people on Earth.

I've always dreamed of this moment, to perform my own little stand-up comedy show, and I can't believe it's finally happening. My friend from college and I would always joke about doing a show in front of our friend in the school cafeteria, and now I'm about to perform in front of a live audience who paid to be here.

Trevor taps me on the shoulder. "Go ahead, man."

"Now?"

"No, in two seconds."

One, two . . .

I walk onstage and hear people cheering.

"Yeah, Marco!"

"Whoop, whoop!"

About fifty people are seated in front of me, and another twenty stand around the bar.

"This room is the size of my house," I exclaim, laughing, getting the attention of the crowd. All of the people here today are Trevor's friends and family at his mansion in Cape Town. They usually get to hear his new work first before a Netflix special or new world tour.

"Before we get started, I want to say thank you first to Trevor. This means a lot to me, and I appreciate you for all the support! Another big thank you to all of you here who are willing, or maybe even forced—that's the likelier option—to listen to me today."

I hear some chuckling.

"You know, as a little kid, I would find a quiet spot some-where in the house, and I would perform to my imaginary audience. The jokes were probably bad, but I was into it, and I would crack myself up. In my opinion, comedy is life." I pause, lowering the mic as the crowd cheers in agreement. "If you don't like comedy and especially stand-up comedy, then something is wrong with you! I mean, it makes you smile, laugh, and you can even learn new things. What else do you need?"

I raise my hands in a shrug.

"If you don't like those things, are you human?" I look around. "No, you're not."

The people laugh.

"A little bit about myself. I grew up in a bunch of different places, and through the company I used to run with my dad, I went to a bunch more places. Many places plus many places equal no places. I grew up with many different languages around me. We would speak English at home. But when we were in Spain, we spoke Spanish and Catalan in school and anywhere outside." Which language am I missing? Oh. "We also spoke French sometimes with my mom since she was French, and every time we visited our grandparents in France, we spoke only French. And I took German classes in almost every school and every grade, so I can speak a little German."

The space distracts me again, and I take in everything. Pool table and Ping-Pong tables in the back. Huge TVs to the right. In the middle, comfortable chairs and sofas.

"Anyway, when you're young, you don't get what knowing multiple languages means, but, Jesus, life is easier when you don't have to wave your hands around!"

I wonder if they are impatient about my first joke.

"But as some of you probably already know, shit can get confusing. I'll give you an example. In Spain, my mom picked my siblings and me up from school at five o'clock."

This stage is much smaller than the one I was on for the TED Talk, but I'm committed to walking left and right. That's what I do when I'm getting into it.

"It's obviously busy because everyone and their mother is picking up their kids. You know the usual stop-and-go traffic. Kids flying around, thinking they have some special Avengers body armor that will protect them from cars."

I get a smile from Trevor. That's good.

"This one lady with her kids crosses the street in front of us, and I see my six-year-old sister staring at her."

I look directly at a lady in the room to add a visual to my story, and I can tell she's getting uncomfortable by the blush on her face and her nervous glances around.

"That's literally how she was staring at her, and my sister says"—I imitate my sister's voice—"'She is embarrassed!'

"I nod my head and reply, 'Yep, she is.'

"My mom was like, 'Who?'" I frown, trying to imitate her confused face. "My mom didn't even know what to think or say because how could my sister and I read a stranger's emotions in a crowd?" I turn my head over my shoulder, pretending I was back in that scene looking at my sister. "My tough, feisty little sister isn't backing down. She points." I extend my right index finger toward the crowd as if the lady was there. "The lady is on the other side of the street now.

"'Right there!'" I imitate her little frustrated and angry face. "She was absolutely not giving up until we understood that the lady on the other side of the street was embarrassed."

I pause and reminisce with a big smile.

"My mom cracks up, and she tells my sister calmly, 'Maria, she is not embarrassed. She is pregnant.'"

The crowd laughs. Either they know Spanish and know what she meant, or they are just in a good mood.

"In my mind, what my sister said never seemed wrong because I knew exactly what she meant to say. My thought process had already done all the necessary translations."

I make eye contact with some of the people in the audience. This time, no blinding lights hit my face.

"I was thinking in Spanish and translated the Spanish word *embarazada* into the English word *embarrassed* and associated it with the pregnant woman crossing the street."

I pause. Overall, I think this mini-story has gone well.

"I connected the dots together in my head. It's pretty cool how bilingual or multilingual minds automatically fill holes or correct 'mistakes' without even consciously thinking."

I point to my head.

"My sister basically *Englishified* a Spanish word that has a completely different meaning in English than the one she was thinking of. Because *embarrassed* was a word she knew actually existed, it sounded right to her."

I gesture with my hands to illustrate an explosion taking place in my brain.

"Absolute genius, isn't she? At least it wasn't the other way around. Imagine telling a woman who is red and sweating from embarrassment that she is pregnant."

The crowd laughs hysterically.

"If you were that child's parent, *you* would be embarrassed."

I laugh a little at my own joke.

"I am sure all of you here appreciate linguistics and also have funny stories you try not to remember too often. Languages are fun, not just because of the unique things about each language or the connections you can make with people, but most importantly because they widen your options for potential partners! In all seriousness and for your own safety, carefully select words you completely understand, and you'll be fine."

I feel good about how it is going with the crowd engaged. Nervousness gone. On to the next story.

"Moving around as often as we did and going to a ton of schools in twelve years made me self-conscious, even borderline paranoid, about certain differences between cultures. The whole mental game about what people do—and don't do—in one place and elsewhere just confused me about life. Greeting people, for example, as simple as it is—and I know you are like, 'How can you screw that one up?'—can quickly get tricky. If I could wish for anything in the world, I would wish that we universally agree on one form of greeting because I just can't seem to get it right."

I shake my head.

"And that's a terrible thing because we live in a world of first impressions, and starting off wrong is awkward."

I pretend to be thinking back in time with a smile on my face.

"So there is the handshake, the air kiss on one cheek"—I'm counting with my hands as I say them—"the air kisses on both cheeks, the simple *hey* hand motion, the head-bowing with the hands together, the sticking out your tongue."

Some people raise their eyebrows curiously.

"I was surprised at that one too, but people in Tibet actually do that, and they have since the ninth century. Fun fact: at the time, they had an unpopular king named Lang Darma who had a black tongue. The belief was that the king had been reborn, and for the people to prove they weren't the king, they would stick out their tongue."

I point at someone in the crowd. "Hi. What's your name?"

"Sean."

"Sean, stick out your tongue, please." I smile.

Sean sticks out his tongue. It's pink.

"Good, you're not the king."

Everybody laughs.

"Just wanted to make sure!"

I continue with the list.

"In Malaysia, you put your hand on your heart. I like that one. Great way to start any conversation because it can only be a loving interaction from there on. You know what? We should definitely adopt that one. Imagine how many arguments we would avoid if people first had to put their hand on their hearts. I mean, come on now. How can you hate when you are aware of the heart? Just saying.

"And in Greenland and Tuvalu, they literally sniff each other's faces. Now, if we adopted that one"—some people in the audience grimace—"wait, hold up, I see some of you not liking that one. I get it. Your face probably does not smell that good." I get some laughs for that one. "If we adopted that one, then I think people would be forced to be cleaner.

Kind of like how flu season gets people to wash their hands for the first time all year."

The crowd is laughing more frequently now. This is a good group of people because even the best stand-up comedians sometimes get the wackiest reactions, like having an audience so quiet it's like they are allergic to laughing.

"My problem with greetings is that, at times, I forget which greeting belongs to that culture and situation. And this is the case even when going back to places I have lived for a considerable amount of time."

It's crazy.

"Some years back, I visited friends in Barcelona and stayed at my friend Pedro's house. We were really good friends in middle school. We stayed in touch over the years, and at the time of the visit, it had already been over five years since I'd left the school."

I don't remember now if my mini show had a time limit. Welp! No stopping now.

"And so, when we got to his house from the airport—his mom, he, and our mutual friend picked me up—their cleaning lady was there. So, of course, Pedro and his mom, Manuela, introduced me to her."

I pause and take a sip of water from the glass on the stool close to me, trying to make this a little bit more dramatic.

"Knowing that Spaniards love to kiss each other, I gave her a kiss on a cheek, and as I was pulling back, she turned." I twisted the side of my face to imitate her position. "I knew I had effed up! She stood there, right cheek presented, with her eyes closed." I rub my forehead with a smile. "I was dying of embarrassment, and I turned red. I tried to fix the situation by giving her the second kiss, but by then, the damage had been done."

Just thinking back on it is embarrassing.

"I forgot that in Spain, the standard way of greeting a lady is with two kisses. One on each cheek. But of course, even after having lived there for seven years, I *completely* forgot. Moral of the story is that the more you know about cultures, the higher your likelihood of screwing up. But as long as you stay alive, you're good."

A sip of water. Second mini-story complete. One more to go.

"This next experience I am going to tell you about was a more significant screwup. Well, at least it was for the other person. It has to do with how people around the world view life differently. I've lived in a country where everything is chill. Live a good life, don't stress too much, and make sure to take your midday nap—you guessed it, Spain. And then I've lived in Germany."

The crowd starts laughing.

"Oh, come on, that's messed up." I mimic Trevor's voice. "But it was a huge change for me. A complete culture shock, and this happened in middle school when I didn't really understand the differences that exist everywhere. From laid-back Spaniards to uptight, formal, driven Germans. In Spain, you call almost everybody by their first name, including teachers. Crazy, right?"

I notice one person who has probably been to Spain and Germany based on his guffaws and facial expression—the one people make when they understand a shared experience others can't quite appreciate.

"But in Germany, it's a whole different story. Of course, you call people you're not bros with by their last name, but unlike in English, where there is only one pronoun for *you*, in German, there are two. *Du* is informal, and *sie* is formal.

German has a whole different pronoun for the formal way of saying *you!*"

Trevor smiles. He speaks some German.

"It was a challenge to not be informal because I was so used to it in Spain. On top of that, my German wasn't even the best. My fourth language, in my defense."

I make a guilty face.

"So twice, I accidentally say *du* when I meant *sie*. Yep! The first time"—I puff—"it must have been the first week of class."

Some laughter.

"It's English class, and my initial feeling of the teacher is that he is a cool older guy. He would always come to class with his leather jacket on. I had a class with him in every one of the three years I was at that school."

Another sip of water.

"So I'm in his class sitting in the back. In the first week, I was not that type of new kid that would march straight to the front. He said something, but I didn't really hear it, so I asked him if he could repeat it again. *Kannst du das nochmal sagen?* The whole class hushed as if they were giving me a minute of silence."

Some seconds go by.

"Finally, the first guy I met in this school explains to the teacher that I'm foreign, and some other classmates add on."

Internally, I am confused. I don't understand what is going on.

"The teacher looks at me with a friendly smile and says, 'I understand in English it is different.'

"A light bulb went off in my head, and I immediately understood the mistake. I felt relieved by the teacher's words. I apologized and went home later that day telling myself it would never happen again."

I smile. The crowd knows exactly where I'm going.

"A week goes by."

Some more laughter.

"I'm in math class now with a different teacher."

Dramatic pause.

"I accidentally committed the same crime, but this time it was worse. As soon as I said *du*, chills went down my back. My life was over. A bunch of people piled on to defend me again, but she wasn't happy."

I look at a few people in the crowd, reminiscing on what felt like life-ending events as a child that are laughable when I think about them now. I really thought something bad—like getting kicked out of the school—was going to happen. Ha.

"Later that afternoon, my mom picks my siblings and me up. She tells me the math teacher wants to have a meeting with her and my dad. In my mind, I am like, *This is the end.*

"But my mom tells me, 'Don't worry about it. Everything will be fine.'"

I make a face of shock. "When parents tell you not to worry about something, that's when you know life is good, because that does not happen too often. Having your parents on your side? Beautiful feeling! At the end of the day, was I wrong? Yes. Was I trying to be disrespectful to her? No, but you can't assume people will want or need to understand your intentions. This teacher was not open-minded, and she did not get or want to appreciate that we are not all from the same place. Yes, it is always important to be cognizant of the various norms and traditions of a country and culture, but in my opinion, you also have to have the flexibility to realize that mistakes can happen. I accidentally said *du* instead of *sie*. Fortunately, I was not kicked out of school, and I never made the mistake again. Thank you very much!"

Everyone claps, and then it quiets down as I walk back into the crowd.

"Great job, Marco!" a couple people tell me.

That was fun!

CHAPTER 13

———

Trevor made me realize I needed to become more social again. When I went to his house, that was the first time in a long while I was really enjoying myself and having a great time. I was smiling and laughing, and, late that night in my room, I almost wanted to cry because I had forgotten how good it felt to be happy.

I told myself I would put effort into reaching out to people and going out more, which is something I was not good at before everything went downhill. But if I wanted things to be different, I knew I had to initiate the change.

After the funeral and spending some time with my dad and sister, I moved to Paris, France. I came here many times while still with the company because we have an office here, and I always loved coming to this beautiful city. This country has some of the world's most iconic landmarks, world-class art and architecture, sensational food, stunning beaches, glitzy ski resorts, beautiful countryside, and a lot of history. I told myself eventually I would come back to live here, even if just for a short time.

I still travel a lot these days, but it's mostly to partici-pate in charity events, work with nonprofit organizations as well as private or public companies, and collaborate with government officials at different levels to help solve some of the biggest issues they face.

A few months ago, I was attending an event in London, England, similar to the one I'm at today, and it was hosted by J. Lo and A-Rod. Many famous people were in attendance— LeBron James, Brad Pitt, Lewis Hamilton, and many more. I had met some of these superstars before, but not that many all at once. Ever since, I have continually looked forward to who I'll meet or see again.

Besides wondering who I'll see, I'm always thinking about what type of food they are going to have. This one has a lot of seafood with lobster rolls, sushi, octopus, you name it. Right as I grab a plate, someone taps me on the shoulder. I turn around, and it's Will. The one and only Will Smith with his big old smiling self.

"Wassup, Marco?"

I immediately put my plate down and give him a hug with my stuffed mouth. After a few seconds, I finally swallow my delicious bite of the lobster roll. "Will! Where'd you come from?"

He grins. "Same place everyone else comes from."

"You're stupid." I laugh. It's always good to see him.

"I just got here a few minutes ago." This guy is looking sharper than he usually does, and he already looks sharp on the regular. Looks like a brand-new red suit and shiny black shoes. I'm wearing a suit I've worn over a hundred times by now.

"Wow, lucky me. I am one of the first people you are talking to, huh?" We both laugh. "Oh, okay, how've you been? Working on a new movie?"

I point to the big plate with the lobster rolls, and he grabs one. "Busy, busy, man. Finished one production a couple months ago, and I'm writing a script for my next one."

"Grind never stops, huh?"

"Nope, and I want you to be a part of it." He gives me this side-eye with a cheesy smile.

"Part of what?" I ask, completely shocked.

"That's the reaction I was expecting," he tells me as he puts his hand on my shoulder. "I want you to be the protagonist of my next movie."

Will is so funny. "You joke around too much," I tell him.

"Nah, I think you are the perfect fit for the role," he says with a straight face.

He must be delusional. It's like saying I'm the perfect person to be Barcelona's striker. Never!

"Will, you just got here. How are you already drunk?"

"I am not drunk."

He really thinks he's funny. "I've never acted before in my life," I say, "and not even as the person in the background you can't even spot."

"Didn't you tell me once you were in a water commercial as a kid?" Will's acting like he caught me in a lie.

"Really, Will? That was not acting. All I had to do was sip from a bottle of water, and my part was a whole two seconds."

"That's experience."

Yeah, right, experience. Jesus, I never thought I would have to bring sense to this man. "Your movies are blockbusters."

"Yep." Straight-faced Will is on display again.

"They're big-time movies." I sweep my hands, trying to make him understand the grandiosity.

"Yep."

This man's gone insane, and I need some more food. So shrimp tempura sushi it will be. "You think putting in a rookie is good for your reputation?"

He puts his hand on my shoulder again, and I am not sure if he's acting funny or serious. "Absolutely. If anything, it will raise my reputation as a director. Marco, trust me. I know what I'm doing."

A couple of people walk by and wave. I return the wave. Anyway, back to Will. "Alright, just to make sure, you are not joking, right?"

"Nope."

Let me go along with whatever this is. "So what is this movie about?"

"It's a modern spy movie."

"Like James Bond?" I smirk.

Will is disappointed in my response. "No. Come on, Marco. You think I'm just going to recreate one of the most famous movie series of all time?"

"So it's a unique spy movie?"

He gives me that face like, *Obviously, dummy.* "Of course it is, and I want you in it because my spy is multicultural and speaks many languages."

"Coincidence?"

"I guess you could say that."

"What else can you tell me?" I grab a few white chocolate-covered strawberries. These things are huge.

"I'm still working on the script, but once it's done, you'll get the full copy."

"Right." I nod.

"And at that point, we'll discuss payment, length of camera rolling time, locations, and more. As far as the name of the movie, I want to talk to you about that too."

This guy had it all planned out. "Did you know I was going to be here tonight? Because you came prepared, so you might as well get it out now."

"I need your permission, though." Will looks at me like I'm his dad forbidding him to play with his friends.

"Why?"

"I would like to call it *The Foreign National*."

"Look, Will, I respect you a lot. You're a great friend, but you just bombarded me with a bunch of crazy stuff in less than ten minutes." These strawberries are the juiciest ones I have ever had.

"What do you think?"

"As of right now, I don't think I want a spy movie to be associated with *The Foreign National*."

Will's slight disappointment turns into one of perseverance. "Once I have the full script written, it will make sense to you. How about this? Once I'm done with the script, I'll send it to you, and we talk about it again?"

I can work with that.

"We can do that. No promises, though." I point to the strawberries and give him a thumbs-up.

"Sounds good." He sounds relieved.

"Alright, Will. I have to speak to some people."

"Talk to you soon, Marco."

I walk to the other tables with food. Can't miss out on this.

EIGHTEEN MONTHS LATER.

"Final touches?" says the assistant director.

"Finals are done," the costume and makeup person agrees.

"Camera ready?" asks the AD.

"Ready," confirms the cameraman.

"Quiet on set!" the AD shouts.

Why don't we just get into it? All these extra checks and yelling back and forth are making me more nervous.

"Roll sound!" yells the AD.

"Sound is speeding," says Juan, the sound assistant.

"Scene one, take eight," announces the AD, followed by the sound of the sticks clapping from the camera assistant.

This scene takes place on a Friday night at a famous jam-packed bar in Barcelona. My character is sitting in the corner all the way in the back with my character's girlfriend. This location gives my character a perfect view of everything going on from the entrance, all the way in the front, the kitchen to the right, all the people around me, and an exit out the back just a few feet away.

"Set," says the camera operator.

"Background," says the AD. At this point, I could have taken a nap.

"Action!" exclaims the director.

My character's conversation is interrupted by the waitress bringing some *tapas* (Spanish appetizers). *Croquetas*, olives, *calamares*, and bread smeared with tomatoes and olive oil with *jamón ibérico* on top. I'm looking around the bar, analyzing people's behavior. Julia, the Spanish beauty who is my character's girlfriend, impatiently wants to speak to me.

"Will you be staying this time?" Julia kicks off the dialogue.

I take a sip of the wine and frown. "You know the answer to that."

"How much longer, François! I can't take this anymore." She pulls out a cigarette.

"It will soon end, my love. Just be patient." I smile gently and resume my observations.

"You've said that for the past three years." She slams her fist on the table. "You never tell me when you are coming! You never tell me when you are leaving! I—"

"Waiter! More wine, please!" I interrupt Julia.

"Coming right now, sir."

"Thank you." I turn my focus back to Julia. "My love, I've told you many times—telling you ahead of time is a great risk to both of us. It's for your own good, and I am tired of having the *same* conversation with you every time. Please just trust me!"

"François, maybe you are fine about having this type of relationship, but I am not. Enough is enough! I can't take it anymore."

Heads are turning. Not good. Not good. Not good. My character bows his head and sighs. *She's right. How much longer is this mission going to take? Which country will it be tomorrow?* Could be Fiji, for all he knows.

"Please, Julia. I'm so close... one more month."

"I don't care. I'm done!" She grabs her purse, gets up, turns around, and as soon as she stalks toward the front exit door, shots are fired into the bar.

I go to the ground, quickly move toward Julia, pull her by the leg, and drag her toward the back exit.

"Julia, you okay?" I ask as she turns toward me.

She nods.

"Follow me!" We get up and run out the back exit.

"He's in the back! Get him!" a man at the entrance shouts.

"Cut!" says the director. "Nice. Print that."

"Moving on," says the assistant director.

Finally. Only took eight takes.

"Alright. First set in the books, guys. Are we excited?" says the assistant director as he turns to everyone behind the scene. He's greeted with happy shouts and enthusiastic clapping.

"The movie has officially begun!" exclaims the director.

More yelling and excitement from everyone. A sigh of relief for me. That was the first scene.

"Alright. Quick fifteen-minute break and then set two starts," adds the assistant director.

I turn toward a little tent about fifty feet away from the set where they have the snack and drinks. I need to moisten my mouth a bit.

"Hey, Marco, come over here," says the director right as I am walking away.

Come on now. I just want some water.

"Yes, Will?" I huff, licking my mouth and lips to remove some of the dryness.

"How do you feel?" he asks me with a hopeful look in his eyes.

"Better and better with every take. I think after a few more scenes, I'll be very comfortable."

"That's good. Keep it up, man. You're going to love this." He grabs my shoulder and gives me an encouraging pat.

"Appreciate it, and thanks for the opportunity." I truly mean it, and I want him to know that.

"I was trying to tell you, but at least you listened to me."

I laugh. He's rubbing it in.

"I'll catch you later though, Marco. I gotta get ready for this next set." He gives me one last encouraging smile and jogs off, script in hand.

I'm not in the next two sets, thank God. Fourth one, though, I'm up again.

And that was the start of my unexpected appearance in the movie world.

CHAPTER 14

———

Not many things, if any, make me feel better than when I am helping other people, and so my dad and I decided to create a charity triathlon tour. The triathlon is composed of sixteen charities, and although they are mainly hosted in underdeveloped countries, some are in developed ones. He did many triathlons in his twenties, thirties, and forties, and I just started my journey now with a few under my belt.

The cause for this one is to fight against climate change by preserving the nature of the local culture, creating new parks and adding more fauna in general, and also helping local businesses (small, medium, and large) convert to net-zero emissions. All proceeds of the event go toward this.

The first triathlon is in New Zealand because that is where my dad did his personal best time for an Ironman, which is a longer form of triathlon. As part of the buildup to the event, my dad was asked to write an article in the *New Zealand Herald* about his first triathlon in Paris.

Below is the article headline.

Don't Ever Swim in a Freezing, Filthy River in Speedo Shorts
The harsh awakening of a rookie triathlete.

I was in beautiful Paris. I had been there for a year already, playing semipro tennis. It was January 4 and freezing cold outside. Nothing was better than being inside, nice and warm, and reading my favorite newspaper, *L'Equipe*. An international triathlon was going to be here in Paris in a few weeks, and some big stars of the sport would be there. They mentioned a triathlete named Marc Allen, who was one of the founders of the sport. If I participate and maybe see this legend, that was reason enough for me to go.

The article said it was an invitation-only field and gave a telephone number for late entrants. I called and said I wanted to register for the triathlon. I mentioned I was American, and that was all it took for them to think I was somebody special to have come all this way to compete in Paris. I borrowed a ten-speed bike from a friend, and I was really looking forward to this new challenge. The distance was called "Olympic," which seemed doable. A three-quarter-mile swim, a forty-kilometer bike ride, and a ten-kilometer run to finish. The swim was going to be fifteen hundred meters in the Seine River, which made me think I was out of my mind to swim in that polluted, dirty body of water, but if pros from all over the world were doing it, then so could I.

It was only when I arrived at the bike staging area the day before that I realized how high-tech this sport was. Every bike I saw had state-of-the-art disc wheels, triathlon handlebars, bladed frames—you name it, they had it. It was cool to see so many people doing a sport that a lot of my friends thought was for masochistic people. However, everyone looked focused but relaxed, sharing laughter and doing their last bag and equipment checks before the big day. I was quite lucky to have been accepted into this event, and I intended to make the most of it.

On the morning of the event, around 6:00 a.m., it was dark, and I got my first surprise as we checked in for the swim start. Everyone had a wet suit on! I was the only triathlete who did not wear one. I had Speedo swim trunks, and it was chilly out. I noticed a few side looks from the athletes, probably thinking either this guy is a badass or lost. The real shock to my system was getting in the icy water, which was nothing like the heated indoor city pool. To make matters worse, we had to tread water for at least fifteen minutes before they got everyone in the water, spread out behind the start banner stretched across the Seine River. By the time the gun went off, I was already experiencing some form of hypothermia.

When the starting gun finally did go off, things went from bad to worse. I was overwhelmed by thrashing arms and legs, pulling and kicking at anything in their way. In that first frenzy of swimmers trying to detach themselves from the pack, I thrashed along, trying to keep my head up, but couldn't avoid drinking nasty river water with almost every stroke. Time seems to stop in life-or-death situations, which is what that swim felt like. After the pack accelerated away and I was more or less on my own, I knew I had bigger problems. I could feel the pores in my body bleeding, my body heat decreasing, and numbness was taking over. That scared me into kicking harder to stave off the cramps I could feel affecting my toes, feet, and calves. I was never happier to see the bright end of anything until I saw the swim banner on the opposite side of the Seine. The problem was that my legs were so weak, it took me a couple of tries to crawl up the moss-covered, slippery cobblestone slope to get to my bike.

As I stumbled to my feet and looked around, a sinking feeling hit me. My bike was the only one left of the hundreds that were parked there earlier. Had I really come out of the water last? My next thought was embarrassment. As I ran to my bike, I could see the press was still there covering the event, and it stunk that I was last. On top of that, for security reasons, the last person was followed by a police motorcade to keep the streets free of cars and people as we passed through. Once the initial wave of feeling sorry for myself passed, my only thought was to push hard on the bike and not be the last person. That thought gave me renewed purpose, and one by one, I started passing riders ahead of me. My confidence was back, and it felt good to be out there doing something crazy and enjoying it.

I felt better about myself when we made it back to the bike park to start the run. It even felt like a victory now that I had gained ground on the bike. Running has always been one of my stronger disciplines, but I never ran ten kilometers after a hard swim and bike event. Your legs feel like rubber and are numb for the first kilometer. You just have to get the circulation going in the right muscles, but it can be frightening for a beginner triathlete because it feels like you have no gas in the *tank with ten kilometers in front of you. Fortunately, my legs responded well, and it felt good to compete in a world-class event, working my way through the field one person at a time.*

I was hooked from that moment on.

That is the article my dad wrote, and some of it was even new information to me. Our charity triathlons are not world-class events but instead are for people with a passion for swimming, cycling, running, and most importantly, our climate and environment.

The fun begins tomorrow.

CHAPTER 15

A YEAR AND A HALF AFTER THE NEW ZEALAND TRIATHLON.

Sometimes in life, you lose your cool but let it out through things like running a little harder, lifting a few more weights, or screaming. In some cases, a person's true colors come out and reveal an ugly side you have never seen before.

I have always been a calm and laid-back person, but I can get intense because of my competitive drive. When I am with my close friends, I get excited and sometimes even loud, but most people would categorize me as a quiet person. These people have only seen me as the guy walking fast from one place to another, looking straight forward.

When I lost my mom after already losing my brother, my personality changed. I got frustrated easily and quickly. Little things that would have never bothered me before were now a big deal.

Long story short, my frustration flared on December 12, which would land me in the courts for a sentencing hearing for eight months.

***

The bailiff kicks off the court session.

"All rise." She waits for everyone except the judge to stand. "Department One of the Superior Court is now in session. Judge Mila presiding. Please be seated."

From her long arms and slim, tall upper body, Judge Mila looks like she played basketball in college. I would imagine she's at least as tall as me at six feet, three inches, maybe even taller.

"Good morning, ladies and gentlemen. Calling the case of the people of the State of North Carolina versus Marco Gaumond. Are both sides ready?" This lady doesn't seem to have many emotions. She's very matter-of-fact from the tone of her voice.

"Ready for the people, Your Honor," says the district attorney. He looks energetic. It will be a huge deal for him if he wins this case.

My defense attorney is prepared too. "Ready for the defense, Your Honor."

"Will the clerk please swear in the jury?" the judge asks, nodding toward the jury, who all look eager to get started.

"Will the jury please stand and raise your right hands?" the clerk instructs, waiting for the jury members to stand again. "Do each of you swear that you will fairly try the case before this court and that you will return a true verdict according to the evidence and the instructions of the court, so help you God? Please say 'I do.'"

One by one, the jurors say, "I do."

"You may be seated," the clerk finalizes, turning back toward the judge.

The prosecution will begin with his opening statements, and then my lawyer will step in right after. I wonder what kind of evidence they are going to present.

"Your Honor"—the deputy DA stands up and first addresses the judge and then faces the jury—"and ladies and gentlemen of the jury, the defendant has been charged with aggravated assault. The defendant violently beat an innocent man into unconsciousness and broke his jaw. Video captured at the moment the incident took place clearly demonstrates behavior that must be condemned under the law and, if I may add, should be charged for attempted murder. In addition to his broken jaw, the victim suffered severe brain damage and was in a coma for several days. The defendant is guilty of the charges. Thank you."

My lawyer clears her throat before standing. I know she is good at her job from her track record, and I'm guessing what she's about to say will prove that.

"Your Honor and ladies and gentlemen of the jury, under the law, my client is presumed innocent until proven guilty. During this trial, you will hear no real evidence against my client. You will come to know the truth: Marco Gaumond was protecting himself. I need to remind you that this altercation occurred after my client was repeatedly harassed, insulted, threatened, and physically pushed on numerous occasions. After enduring this for a considerable amount of time, my client had every right to defend himself. Furthermore, after finding out that the other person was unconscious, my client called 911 to provide medical aid to his tormentor as soon as possible. Marco cooperated with all parties involved every step of the way. He has been transparent from the beginning. For all these reasons, my client is not guilty."

After evidence is presented from both sides, the court is adjourned to reconvene in a few days for the jury's turn to decide the case.

***

How do I feel? Empty. I feel so empty thinking of what this sentence could mean to me. I'm numb, but not because I don't care about possibly going to prison. It's because I have hit another low point in my life.

I thought my mental issues when I was barely a teenager were bad. Losing my brother was even worse, and then losing my mother has been too much to handle.

Only when you think life is worth living are you scared about a sentence.

***

The three days pass, not slowly, not quickly, they just do, and I find myself shuffled back into the courtroom. After quick pleasantries and formalities, the judge continues.

"Are you ready with final arguments?" Judge Mila looks at both attorneys.

"Yes, Your Honor," says the deputy DA.

"Yes, Your Honor," agrees my attorney.

Finally, almost at the finish line.

The deputy DA stands up and faces the jury. "Your Honor and ladies and gentlemen of the jury, the judge has told you we must prove three things. There is absolutely no question about the first and third things. From the video footage, we clearly see the defendant not only punched the victim but went way beyond a single punch. He repeatedly, one after another, smashed the victim with his fists. The defendant was undoubtedly trying to seriously hurt, if not kill, the victim. Twelve punches total." He paused dramatically. "Think about that," he says, making careful eye contact with each of the jurors. "The fact that the victim is even alive today is an act of God," he reveals, receiving a few hushed murmurs in response.

Bringing religion into it, I see.

"Therefore, all we have to prove is that the victim did *not* harass and threaten the defendant. We know the defendant was slightly drunk. Tests conducted at the scene prove this. We also know that the two had a brief discussion before entering the view of the camera. The victim has clearly stated from the beginning that Marco provoked him to begin the altercation. That shows that the defendant initiated the confrontation and not the victim. Based on the evidence, you must find the defendant guilty."

The deputy DA sits down. Of course, he left out all his client's harassment and the fight he started. But it's now my attorney's turn. Maybe she'll bring that up.

My attorney stands up and faces the judge and then the jury. "Your Honor, ladies and gentlemen of the jury, both parties were unlucky to get into a fight. However, as the video footage clearly demonstrates, the victim undoubtedly harassed, taunted, and threatened Marco not just once but for two full minutes. The defense has demonstrated Marco's character as calm, collected, and thoughtful, and it is very—I repeat, *very*—hard to get him even slightly disturbed. Marco is twenty-three now, and he has been in the spotlight for more than half of his lifetime. Not once has he been in a fight or done anything against the law or even indicated that he has tried to undermine the law. He has always been a law-abiding citizen of this country, and his record is completely clean. There is absolutely no reason to believe Marco wanted to seriously hurt the victim and even less reason to believe he would want to kill someone. The prosecution has presented no real evidence to prove all three things mentioned by the prosecutor beyond a reasonable doubt. That means that you must find him *not guilty*."

"Ladies and gentlemen of the jury," the judge begins. "I am now going to read to you the law you must follow in deciding this case. To prove the crime charged against the defendant, the prosecution must prove three things to you: First, that the defendant punched the victim. Second, that the victim did not harass and threaten the defendant, and therefore the defendant did not act in self-defense. Third, that the defendant intended to violently hurt and/or kill the victim.

"If each of you believes the prosecution proved *all three* of these things beyond a reasonable doubt, then you should find the defendant guilty. But if you believe the prosecution did not prove any *one* of these things beyond a reasonable doubt, then you must find the defendant *not* guilty.

"Proof beyond a reasonable doubt does not mean beyond all possible doubt. It means you are very sure, considering all of the evidence, the charge is true."

The judge sits back, showing she is finished speaking. After the bailiff's quick instruction, the jury exits the room to discuss their verdict.

After some minutes, they reenter, a range of mixed emotions showing on their faces. A few look confident, others pleased, and one or two look downright nervous.

"Will the jury foreperson please stand?" asks the clerk. "Has the jury reached a unanimous verdict?"

The foreperson says, "Yes."

The clerk reads out the sentencing. "The jury finds the defendant... not guilty."

Judge Mila offers a final closing statement. "The jury is thanked and excused. Court is adjourned."

Wow. I'm not guilty.

I think about what this means, and it's only after hearing those words I realize how relieved I am that this didn't end the other way.

***

I walk out of the courthouse about thirty minutes later with my lawyer, and cameras are everywhere. I see my dad, and I give him a big hug. I look around for my sister, but my dad's expression tells me she didn't come. I don't blame her.

"I'll take him home," he tells my lawyer.

"Sounds good, sir," she says. "Well, Marco, call us if you need anything."

"Will do. Thank you very much!" I say, surprising myself.

"You're welcome. We'll stay in touch in case anything arises."

My dad turns to me with a serious look on his face. "I'll take you home," he states again, pushing me by the back.

After not eating anything this morning because of all the emotions, I am now hungry. "Can we stop at the café and get a sandwich?"

"No, I have food in the car. No need for you to spend more time outside today."

For half of the ten-minute car ride to my dad's apartment, he remains quiet. I was starting to think he wasn't going to say anything at all until he pierced the air with, "You were very lucky."

I don't say anything. I know he has more to say.

"Just because the verdict was in your favor does not mean you were right."

"I know I wasn't."

"You better watch out because next time, you'll be in jail."

"But he provoked me," I complain.

"So? Is that the first time you've had someone in your face? No, it's not! Everybody knows who you are, and not everybody wants to see you succeed. He purposefully did what he did, and you know that, and your dumb ass decided to knock the shit out of him!"

My eyes start watering. It must have been three years since I cried last. The same pain is coming back.

"Are you still going to your therapist?" asks my dad.

"No." I'm sobbing.

"Why did you stop going?" My dad looks at me the same way he did when I was little and in trouble.

I shrug. "I don't know."

"First thing you need to do is get back with her. Understood?"

I look down at my hands and notice they are shaking. I don't worry about faking a level of calmness I certainly don't have. After some long seconds, I say, "Yes."

"Just because you think you are okay doesn't mean you stop going. And why did you have to beat him down like that?"

"Because he insulted Mom."

CHAPTER 16

The day after the trial ended, I decided to Airbnb at a house in the boonies. Just me, myself, and I and some time to think about everything.

I sit on a couch by the window that looks out into nature as I scroll through my phone.

"Marco steps down!" a woman says in a video.

That's the headline of every breaking news segment.

Shortly after the verdict, my lawyer advised me to step down as a member of the board of directors of the company I helped build. I don't know why they didn't push it sooner, since my not-guilty verdict did not change anything for me.

I was already distancing myself from the company by stepping down some years ago from the CEO position to focus on my mental health. But I never thought I would be completely removed from the company. My team saw me grow from a little boy into an adult. They saw me travel the world. They saw me in happiness and in sadness. They saw me crumble and flourish. They saw me grow from nobody to the Foreign National. And now, this has all come to an end. An end I had never expected. But heck, as Socrates would say, if I know anything about life, it's that I know nothing.

Do I regret what I did? Absolutely not! You insult my mother, and you get what you get. There is no second-guessing that. Could I have ignored the guy all up in my face until I had had enough? Sure, and I did until he crossed the line. The pain of having lost my mom is still too great for me to ignore someone continuously insulting her. And as a result, I got what I deserved too.

Honestly, I was lucky I didn't have to serve any time in prison because even though a lot of people would have done the same thing I did, it does not make it right. The last thing I want is to promote violence and tarnish the brand I helped create for the company. There were probably some people in the company who wanted to get rid of me just to have their time to shine, but I have no hard feelings toward anyone. I accept the decisions I made, and I hope the best for everyone. Plus, my dad is still involved in the operations of the company.

***

A couple days later, I am participating in a live audio chat room. Recently they have become popular, and that was one of the last big projects I was working on to implement into the website for the company, but for this new hobby, I guess I will be using a different platform.

Even though I should probably be keeping a low profile at this point, I scheduled a live audio chat room for anyone interested in asking me questions. Who cares what people say I should and shouldn't be doing?

***

"Hello, everybody! Thank you for tuning in today for my first live audio chat room. I will do several of these over the coming weeks, and this is your chance to ask me any questions you have.

"Question number one comes from Amber. 'If I ever have FOMO, otherwise known as fear of missing out, what should I do?'

"Amber, as you probably already know—and I think at some point everyone has experienced this—FOMO comes from seeing what someone has now or in the past that other people would want to have too. They don't want to miss out on this perceived opportunity. You know the hindsight bias of knowing a bunch of things and scenarios in retrospect, which alters decisions in the present and thoughts about an ideal future. I definitely used to have FOMO, but I quickly realized that chasing what I thought I could maybe be missing out on would only make me less happy. If you live in the moment and you are consistently working on goals you enjoy, no matter if they are small or big, you won't have FOMO. Stick to your path, and don't worry about that of other people.

"Question number two comes from Juan. 'What do you think about the YOLO lifestyle at a young age?'

"Juan, I am all for fun. Trying new things, you know, as long as it is safe, of course, is great. I did not personally do much of the YOLO things like partying, drinking, traveling, and spending lavishly. The only thing I would say is that when you think of this lifestyle, you think of freedom—doing what you want when you want it without anyone telling you otherwise. And so think about different ways to make your entire life the YOLO lifestyle. Invest your money, start a business, whatever you want to do. Work on it. I see young people graduate from college with nothing much to do because they were only YOLOing their life away. You need a balance.

"Question number three comes from Amy. 'What are some tips you could give people, like myself, who suffer from depression?'

"Good question, Amy, thank you. From a young age, I have been dealing with depression. My dad too. One of the biggest challenges and tips I have is giving yourself some personal time. I have done a bad job of that, and it has affected me negatively. In the past, I have prioritized many things over my well-being, and even if you think, as I did, that your depression is gone, that is when it comes right back at you. So what I do is take at least thirty minutes in the morning and evening to meditate.

"Question number four comes from Emily. 'How can I make a positive change in the world?'

"The biggest possible change you can make, Emily, is in the little daily things you do. I have seen people donate millions of dollars, and yes, there is an initial impact, but not in the long term if it hasn't been thought out well. It's much more than a number. It's how we treat each other that really counts. Education is by far the best way you can make a positive change in the world. Not just you, but anybody, because you need to be educated on a subject to help create social change. It's the little things that make the big things happen.

"This is the fifth and last question, and it comes from Timothy. He asks, 'How do you know what is next in life?'"

That is a good one.

"Honestly, Timothy, you just don't know. The beauty of life is not knowing where it will lead you. Now some people live a prescriptive lifestyle and follow a manual by the book. Go to college, find your partner, get a good job, get married, have children—all in the same town or city. But for other people like me, there is no set next thing to do. I could decide right now what's next and tomorrow, but everything changes. And I am not saying you should not look into the future. You have to, in a sense, have big long-term goals you are working toward. For example, I had financial goals from an early age, so I invested a lot of money into it, knowing I was probably not going to reach that goal in the short term, but I would get to it little by little. So be open and flexible. I know people like certainty, but certainty often limits one's life.

"Well, I appreciate everyone for tuning in. We had a lot of great questions today, and if you weren't able to ask your question, I will be doing another live audio chat in a few weeks."

That was fun. Being able to talk about life. I definitely want to do this more often. Since I was eleven, I have been so busy, I don't even know what I want to do now. I always had something to do. In fact, I had more to do than I could even handle, but now I can do whatever I want when I want. I just hope no major depressive events occur now.

Let's see what is to come...

CHAPTER 17

These days, I like doing runs early in the morning before anyone else is up.

The sound of calm water moving throughout this confined space of this massive lake in Sydney sets up a nice peaceful start to the day.

In the last forty-eight hours or so, my body has not been in sync with the calmness of my surroundings, though.

I run anyway.

Right step, left step, right step…

I feel funny.

I feel my face touching the ground. That's the last thing I remember.

***

"Hi, Marco, how are you doing?" the doctor asks as he walks back into the room.

"Better now, thank you," I tell him, thinking of how much he looks like the doctor I had when I broke my wrist when I was eleven. I glance at his badge but see he has a different name.

"That's great. So we ran a few preliminary tests, and it looks like you have low blood sugar."

Interesting. I have been told in the past I have low blood pressure but never low in sugar.

"We are going to take some more tests to see what may have caused the hypoglycemia, which is the medical term for low blood sugar. One cause could be diabetes. Do you know if you have diabetes?"

Diabetes? "Not to my knowledge. I have never been told that."

"Okay. It is possible to get diabetes later in life, but diabetes is not the only possible reason for hypoglycemia. As mentioned, we will be doing extra tests throughout today and tomorrow, and then we'll check the results."

"Do you think it is anything serious?" I ask, nervous to hear the answer. I keep telling myself to calm down and that everything is fine, but I'm finding that's easier said than done.

"It depends. Hypoglycemia can be caused by many different things, and so after these tests, we'll have a much better picture."

***

LATER THAT DAY.

I don't mind being here in the hospital because I don't need to worry about anything. No people, no calls, no emails, nothing. Just relaxing peacefully by myself.

"I see your son does not have insurance," a nurse tells the family next to me. Just by the tone, I can tell this will be followed by awful news. A family's world is about to fall apart right in front of me, separated by only a thin, flimsy curtain.

"That's correct."

"The total cost for the stay is $30,000, and unfortunately, we will not be able to do the chemotherapy for your son without insurance."

"The doctor said earlier we need to start therapy as soon as possible!" The mom starts to lose it. Her voice is rising and cracking while she cries intensely.

"I understand, ma'am. However, unless you can show us you can pay for chemotherapy, which usually costs at a minimum $100,000 without insurance, we cannot do anything."

"There is absolutely nothing you can do for us?" It sounds like her tears are in her mouth.

"Here, no, but we can transfer your son to a public hospital."

Public hospitals are horrible. That's where I say enough is enough. "*I'll pay!*"

I hear the curtain slide open. My eyes are still closed.

"Sir, were you speaking to us?" says the nurse.

"Yes, I was. I will pay the costs for the kid."

"Are you sure, sir? The total amount could come to over $150,000."

"That number seems to be going up with every second that goes by," I say in a sarcastic voice.

The nurse responds matter-of-factly, "It's because I don't know exactly how much it will be. It depends on many factors."

"I heard the conversation. I have sufficient money to pay."

I hear the mother still weeping profusely. I open my eyes.

"Can I see the boy, please?" I ask.

The nurse opens the curtain fully, and I look to my right. He looks to be about seven and completely frightened. His eyes are watery, and he probably doesn't understand what is going on. I'm sure he would rather just play with his friends. I look at the mom, and I want to scream at the nurse and this fucking health system. The mom is a mess. Her mascara is all over her cheeks. Her eyes are completely red. I close my eyes again and cry internally. Why are we so cruel to each other? Isn't learning your son might die not bad enough news for someone to bear? And they're trying to deny him at least a chance at surviving.

"Please make sure he gets the best treatment you have to offer," I tell the nurse.

I'm guessing she recognizes me because she hasn't asked me for proof that I can pay possibly hundreds of thousands of dollars.

"Yes, sir, we will do our best."

I hear the mom mumbling, but she can't get her words out.

***

On the first evening in the hospital, I had a not-too-bad dinner consisting of fish, rice, and some salad. Now it's time to read a little bit before going to sleep, seated at this stiff chair next to the bed. *Chimpanzee Politics* by Frans de Waal is such a great book.

"Mr. Gaumond," a lady calls my name in a calm and collected voice. Of course, she butchered the pronunciation, but that is okay.

"Yes, that's me." I wasn't expecting any visitors at this time of day.

Gently, the little boy's mother moves the curtain like it was made of the most delicate and precious cloth straight from the Middle East. In the split second that the curtain is open, the boy waves at me. I smile and wave back. The mom closes the curtain and looks at me as if I'm Jesus himself.

"What is your name?" I ask her to break the ice.

"Sorry, my name is Haymar."

She looks to be about five feet seven or so, which was the height of my mom. She has quite a few calluses on her hand and some holes in her clothes, but I can tell she tries her best to look presentable with a good straight posture and touched-up makeup.

"Nice to meet you, Haymar." I get up, push the IV stand with me, and extend my hand to her. "How is your son doing?"

"Better, but he is nervous about the surgeries and the therapy that is going to come."

"Can I say something to him?"

"Yes, absolutely." She calls her son to come over.

"Hey, friend, what's your name?" I ask the boy.

He looks better, too, now.

"Cho."

"Cho, let me tell you everything will be great, okay?"

Cho is shy, but he responds, "Okay."

"Once I finish talking to your mom, we can play some games."

Cho smiles.

His mom lightly taps him on the back. "Cho, give me a second with Mr. Gaumond, please."

"Okay, Mommy," he says and returns to his bed.

"Thank you so much, Mr. Gaumond. I am forever indebted to you."

I put my hand up. I don't like when people say they are indebted to someone. No one is indebted to anyone.

"We're a team, Haymar. If one person is down, the other person has to pick the other one up. I don't need to know you to help you."

"You don't understand the appreciation I have for you," she assures me, obviously not satisfied with my response.

"Tell me your story, Haymar, if you don't mind sharing." I wonder about her background and where her heavy accent comes from.

"Absolutely, sir. My son and I immigrated here about a year ago. We are some of the few Rohingyas who, through luck, were granted asylum here in Australia."

"Oh, that's great!"

"Yes, very lucky. My husband stayed behind to fight, but in all likelihood, he is not doing well now."

"I'm sorry to hear that."

"For us Muslims, things are getting worse in Myanmar."

I have read quite a bit about Myanmar and its history. One of my friends from college is a refugee from Myanmar.

"Have you been able to find work here?" I ask her.

"It's hard, especially since I have my son to take care of too."

"What happened to him?"

"He hasn't been feeling well for over a week, and yesterday it got much worse, so I took him here."

***

The next morning, the doctor told me I would be able to leave in the evening. I had vasovagal syncope, which is a condition that can lead to fainting. It's usually not harmful, and in my case, it was probably triggered by excess heat and prolonged exercise.

Unfortunately, they transferred Cho to the children's section of the hospital in a separate building about a mile away, but I told him and his mom I would stop by once I was released.

For lunch, I was able to go to the little cafeteria they have for the patients, and a group of people invited me to their table. They introduced themselves as Bryan, Trae, Trina, and Jonathan. From what I was told, a person named Jewell used to be a part of the group too, but she passed away a couple of days before I came.

Lunch is over, and we are playing cards.

"Who's shuffling?" asks Bryan, starting the conversation.

It's hangout time, and we're playing the game that breaks friendships, UNO. What an addicting game it is.

"I got it," I say. I'm good with the quick shuffle and the different techniques to do it. I spread the cards. The game is on!

"If you guys could make it a little bit entertaining this time, I would really appreciate it. Thanks," says Bryan.

From the previous games, I can tell he is the smack talker of the group. He told me he used to play D1 basketball, and I can already imagine what type of team member he was. Competitive, in your face, but can back it up. Funny thing is, he is only five feet, eleven inches tall. What he lacked in height, he compensated for elsewhere. As far as his chances of surviving, they are looking dim. He has family who comes every day. Nice people.

"I'll try," Trina says.

You won't get more than a couple of words out of her at a time. She has that intelligent look on her face that makes you think she has an IQ of 200. Does that number even exist? Who cares. Trina has a Ph.D. and was doing research at the university here in Sydney until she was diagnosed with brittle diabetes, a severe and uncommon type of diabetes. No family. I'm surprised she even spends time with us.

"We're going clockwise, which means I get to start," Jonathan, the youngest of the group, declares. I feel bad for him since he just had his nineteenth birthday, and this is not even the first time he's had cancer. He had it already when he was ten. This time around, they didn't find out about it until a more advanced stage. I think he'll make it, though. He never complains, and when his family came to visit for lunch, he was so positive and happy to see them. His mom is pessimistic.

***

You would think being in a hospital is always a depressing place because it is filled with people with all kinds of issues, but these issues are perceived primarily by people on the outside. On the inside, this place is so much fun, at least for me. Chitchatting about our lives, playing games... Sometimes you need a shocker to make you forget about all the worries in life outside and enjoy the present moment, even if it's a hospital visit.

CHAPTER 18

I never thought I would lose my motivation to go after new and big challenges, but now I feel like doing nothing. I couldn't care less about anything. I threw that drive I had and that military schedule I followed to accomplish all the things I wanted to do out the window. I can't seem to have fun anymore, but at least I have money, so I can afford to do nothing for a while. Hopefully, I get out of this slump soon.

***

I reach the door to a twenty-floor apartment complex and buzz a number to be let in. I hear the door unlock, so I push through and head up the stairs until I reach the fourteenth floor. I am not a big fan of elevators because my mom hated them, and so I endure all fourteen flights. When I finally reach the top, I see the door to the apartment I'm looking for is already open, but I don't see anyone inside. I enter the first room to the right and lay on a super comfortable sofa. Eyes closed. I'm ready.

I hear footsteps coming.

"I see you are ready to get started, Marco?"

I have been going to my therapy sessions with Sofia on and off for several years now. Lately, I have been back on the ritual.

"Yep! Today is a great day!"

My eyes remain shut. She doesn't use the psychoanalytic method of therapy, but I still lay back on the couch and close my eyes as if Freud himself was trying to make sense of my dreams.

"Tell me about your day."

"Woke up, ate breakfast, ran a couple of miles, ate some more, watched a movie, took a nap, and came over here with Jo. I might join him for basketball later."

"That's great, Marco, but remember I need your mind to be fully in this session now, and—"

"It is."

I'm sure if I open my eyes at this very moment, she is probably staring at me. I've been kind of cold to her lately.

"Marco, I don't like to bring this up, but it has been a couple of years now since your mom was killed, and you haven't made much progress since then."

I sit up and look her in the eyes. I *am* trying. Not really for myself but for my mom and brother. I am trying for them, which is why I even started going to therapy. But in big moments of my life, I can't control it. I lost hold of my brother, I couldn't reach my mom before she was killed, and now I feel like I am trapped, and I can't get out.

"Are you still taking your medication?"

Absolutely not! Can't stand that stuff.

"Sometimes, yeah."

"Why not as often as I prescribed?"

"I don't know. I just sometimes don't want to."

"The medication is important for your health, Marco."

"I understand, but I forget. I get busy, and then I lose track of the pills."

"Marco, for Christ's sake. You're twenty-six! You've gone through some deep shit, but you need to get it together! All I am asking is for you to take your medication when I tell you. Simple!"

"Ay, wow. Remember, this is a therapy session, and you're my therapist. Can't speak like that."

"Marco, you're trying to be funny now, but you will see! I'm your girlfriend, and that doesn't change whether this is a therapy session or not."

So much for that. I've really been thinking we were some of the best actors out there. Not anymore.

"You just broke the code."

Sofia's face is furious and sad at the same time. I've been with her for a couple years. This is how we met. Through therapy. I fell for her, she fell for me, and here we are. This whole dating your therapist thing has been interesting.

"Marco!"

"Okay, I'm sorry. I'll make sure to take all the medication, and I am really trying to improve. It's hard, though. Let's enjoy our life, Sofia, and worry less."

"You know, Marco, I knew as soon as I saw your name pop up as one of my clients that I should have not accepted it. I should have let someone else become your therapist. You're a cute guy with a great personality, and I know from following your past that you are an unbelievable person. Still, at the same time, your carelessness in some aspects makes it frustrating for a therapist and even more for a girlfriend."

"Are you suggesting something?"

"I'm suggesting you find a new therapist, and we end our relationship. I've tried enough."

Shit, man! I don't understand why my life is like this. Everything always seems to go wrong.

I walk out of the apartment in disbelief.

I don't think love was ever for me, or at least not now. Having someone so close to me, seeing all of my vulnerabilities, is probably not the best thing. I like having relationships with people and helping them with their issues, but I don't like when I'm the one who needs to be inspected and helped. It's weird, I know. You want to help everybody but not get help yourself. Such is life.

I need to figure this out now.

CHAPTER 19

———

I sit on the couch and open the February 16 issue of the *Daily News* for the umpteenth time. Some people threw a bunch of copies right outside my house, maybe to make me aware of this "scandal." Not sure about the motif, but I picked one up anyway.

THE RISE AND DEMISE OF THE FOREIGN NATIONAL. IS THIS ANOTHER CELEBRITY DOWNFALL?
That's the newspaper headline. It has a nice, big picture of me walking out of a club in London's red-light district. My clothes were only half on, despite the early morning, freezing cold winter weather. I had a blunt in my mouth and a bunch of women following closely behind. My face is pale, and I look like I'm on a different planet. I don't remember a single thing from that night, but I sure as heck have that picture embedded in my head now.

***

A MONTH AFTER THE BREAKUP AND A FEW DAYS BEFORE THE COMPLETELY DISGRACEFUL OUTING.

It's 5:00 p.m., and I'm just now rolling out of bed. I can't seem to get out of this funk, and, if anything, it has only gotten worse in the last month. I'm still staying out late, going to bed after breakfast, and only waking up in time for the next stupid thing.

I don't care about anything anymore. I'm tired of life, tired of the microscope on me. Even thinking is tiring these days.

I spend most of my waking hours trying to be somewhere else. Not physically but mentally.

I might be out of joints. Let me check under my bed where I keep everything. Nope, nothing left. Crap, my guy is a hot minute away from where I live, and I don't feel like going there now.

What did he ask me again last time? Oh, yeah. "How are the kids in Croydon?" He only asked me because he likes one of the teachers.

I started there as one of our company initiatives in London for children of disadvantaged immigrant back-grounds. We started it off for one hundred kids, and I think it has grown to about six hundred. I'm not sure of the latest number because I have not been involved in the last year and a half. Even thinking about it now feels like remembering something from a different life.

Anyway, all I wanted from him was my weed and peace.

"They're doing good," I told him absently while looking in the bag. Seeing everything there, I handed him the money.

Right after I left, I remember getting frustrated and angry because a homeless man almost caused me to trip over him.

***

A couple of days later, I am at the club.

I'm at the bar drinking my virgin cocktail when a guy calls my name. I must say, even in all my despair, I have still never had alcohol. That is one of those things I have never wanted, but tonight, that could change.

I don't know this guy, and I'm tired of people coming up to me because I'm famous.

"What's up," I say, annoyed. I wish people would leave me alone. It's a simple request.

"What's wrong with you, man?"

"Excuse me?" I demand. He better not be another one of those people critiquing me for every little blink I make. This won't end well otherwise.

"Are you stupid?" he asks.

"Who the fuck are you?" I shout, jumping up. The guy flinches at my sudden movement and the noise my chair makes as it scrapes backward.

Does this guy really want to start a fight here? One of his friends pulls him back. I turn back to the bar and take some sips from my virgin drink. Screw it. I order a bunch of alcoholic drinks recommended by the bartender, and soon after that, I am gone.

***

A WEEK LATER.

I take a shower and put on some light clothes. I walk to my room and sit at my desk. I have plenty of other rooms for my desk, but having it in my bedroom, as was the case in college, is something I never got away from. To this day, it's still my preferred spot.

It's time to write a letter that has been coming for some time now. Yes, it is time.

Dear family,

This has been one heck of a ride. Who would have thought that an idea my dad had in 2010 would end up becoming a multibillion-dollar company and take us all over the world? Crazy stuff. I might have been twelve, thirteen, fourteen, but I felt like I was the same age as everyone else on the team in their twenties, thirties, forties, and fifties. Those people became my childhood friends. You know we've done a lot of great things. We've helped millions of students around the world connect and improve their education. Our philanthropic efforts are growing exponentially and are basically running themselves at this point. Couldn't be happier about that.

But what I can't be happy about is the devil inside my mind. It's been messing with me for as long as I can remember, but these last few years have been getting worse. I'm embarrassing myself and the people around me, and I'm doing more harm than good in all I have been doing lately. I thought with time, things would get better, but they haven't. It's too much, and I can't do it anymore. I have plenty of money, but guess what? Money can't pay off the devil. He doesn't care about the money. No quantity will satisfy him. I know a lot of people say it is unbearable to live anymore, and that sounds cliché, but there is no other way to describe it. It's simply become unbearable.

Please continue to do all the great things you are doing. I love you from the bottom of my heart.

Marco

I place the envelope in the letter. Lick it, close it.

Peace.

CHAPTER 20

Long story short, I somehow survived my suicide attempt. I remember my eyes forcing themselves to close. Sometime later, they opened again.

I knew if I wanted any chance to live in this world and not end up six feet deep, I had to do something completely different. Something I would have never thought of doing.

I do not know if this happened in reality or in a dream, but I briefly encountered someone who told me I should consider flying to Thailand and becoming a monk.

Nothing in the past had worked, so I booked a one-way flight to Thailand with nothing but a backpack that I would soon not even need anymore.

***

Three years later and today is the big day for me and my journey in Buddhism. If everything goes well and I stand the test, I will become a monk.

With every stroke of the blade, I feel myself getting lighter. I feel this immense relief in my heart. This is me, Atid.

Atid is my new name.

Bzzzz.

There goes my left eyebrow.

Bzzzz.

There goes my right eyebrow.

Bzzzzzzzzzzzzzzzzzzzzzzz.

Done. I'm bald. My hair is gone. Three years ago, on this date, I tried to end my life. Today, I am a monk. I went from a person who did not want to live anymore to a person seeking liberation from the limitations and desires of the physical world. I went from experiencing a constant earthquake in my head to my present state of complete bliss. I am lucky to be here, and I am thankful to have come to this enlightening land.

***

EARLIER THAT DAY.

Yes! I did it. I passed the "test." I am officially a monk. To give a little bit of background information, in the Buddhist monk's code of ethics, which is called the Vinaya, the Buddha decreed that a candidate for higher ordination must have a preceptor, a person who will take care of them throughout his monastic life. Several years ago, at the time of my novice ordination, I begged the senior monk to be my preceptor; the senior monk agreed, so I had him guide me for as long as he remained a bhikkhu (monk) in the Sasana (Buddha's dispensation).

This is by no means the end goal, and I am not sure what the future now holds, but in a way, I do not even care anymore because I am in the present, and the present feels great. This feeling that I have now is the best one that I have ever had, and it is not even close despite all the "successes" people might say I had before things got ugly. The fame, money, connections, business, etc. None of that matters because the most important thing in the world is to be happy and enjoy life. Even though I am starting to like myself better and better now, I don't think I am completely out of the woods yet, but I know I am on the right path.

How long will I be a monk? Will I ever want to become a layperson again? I want to become a layperson again and rejoin the hustling and bustling, but I will not cease being a monk until I have that feeling inside of me of being at peace with myself. Because no matter how materialistic, broken, and corrupt the people around me may be, as long I am in the right state of mind, nothing will be able to bring me down again. This is the start of another chapter in my life, and now I must pay attention to the instructions being given to me concerning the life of the bhikkhu (monk).

***

It has been several months since the day of my higher ordination, and today, I have decided to "let my robes fall to the ground." To be a monk for this short of a period is not unusual, quite the contrary. For some, their goal to become a monk was to challenge themselves to go through the lengthy ordination process. For others, because they are required. I did this all with the goal of becoming a new person at peace with myself. I had no timetable in mind.

I am at peace.

Coincidentally, mere days after I start using my phone again after a months-long hiatus, my dad reaches out to me. He wants to come see me, but with the heavy rain season already underway, I tell him to wait for the weather to be more enjoyable to visit this beautiful country. So we make plans for December.

***

The holiday season has arrived, and my dad is in town. After going for a nice run this morning, we are now walking through the busy Chatuchak Weekend Market in Bangkok.

We are in the most crowded part of the market. There isn't much of a walking path, and many of the stalls lean into this space. I wade through people, seeking openings. We get split up, and my dad is a distance ahead of me.

He turns around, looking for me. "Marco?"

He can't see me. I want to answer, but someone covers my mouth.

"Marco!" He raises his voice.

As I struggle against the unwelcome grip, my head gets dizzy, and my eyes close. The next thing I know, I am in a dark place. I cannot see anything, and I have no clue where I am. I hear footsteps approaching…

Then I'm gone.

ACKNOWLEDGMENTS

———

I would like to thank all my family and friends who have supported me throughout this adventure. Thanks to my parents for introducing me to the beautiful world of books many, many years ago. Special thanks to my friend Joseph Minani who, as an author himself, went through this journey just a year before me. He showed me that it is possible for a college student to write and publish a book and that it can be an amazing experience with the help of the Creator's Institute and New Degree Press. Joseph has been great assistance throughout this time and has helped me in many ways, including filming my book fundraising campaign video (sharing Richard's frustration about my lack of ability to get it right on the first take, ha) and providing me with important tips to successfully reach the campaign goal.

I would like to express my deepest appreciation to all of my backers who contributed to my presale campaign page, making the publication of *The Foreign National* even possible. I received generous support from all of you, including: Sirena Register, Pa Sheikh Ngom, Adriel Solorzano, Martina Muñoz, Eric Margolin, Yojana Rodriguez, Joseph Minani, Quinn Mcleod, Anne Karnbrock, Gary Mcleod, Helena Segabinazzi,

Cristina Martinez, Nicolas Barone, Parashar Ranade, Sabrina Andolpho, Eric Koester, Isis Ferreira, Rose Hemans, Janellé Forbes, Jalyna Ambrocio, Christina Chuba, Hermon Gebrezgiabher, Dr. Jorge Presmanes, Irmadelin Olivier, Dr. Victor Romano, Natasha White, Orianna Camargo, Jeff Lozin, Ryan Barras, Jarlyn Álvarez, Ísaly Ortiz, Tatyana Wimbley, Immanuella Jones, Alan Mcleod, Judisha Williams, Naomi Garcia, Aliana Bennazar, Kaseim Ezell, Matt Cameron, Dr. Karen Stalnaker, Doreen Noel, Jo-Ann Gozaloff, Cristina Herrera, Cherise Key, Luis Garcia Almansa, Rosy Gomez, Vincenzo Esposito, Marietta de Winter, Amponsah Asamoah, Jonathan Dominique, John Victor, Johanssen Grandoit, Daniel Cendan, André Swaby, Tara Marinkovic, Sarah Ruiz, Lilly Mcleod, Shanieya Harris, Britania Cameron, Liz James, Jaynell Pittman, Freddy Brea, Zhonnell Bailey, Kiara Morisseau, Jessica Morency, Dominique Guerrero, Derricha Joseph Taylor, Danyell Baker, Ashley Dever, Alexander Orozco, Sébastien Poulet, Heaven Laster-Torres, Essence Butler, Valencia Martinez, Samantha Ternelus, Jasmine Lockhart, Mayalisa Cousins, Gyanna Guillermo, Rebecca Young, Sidney Burnette, Monika Herrera, Bryce Reddick, Iven Guillot, Paige Pokryfke, Dr. Glenn Bowen, Ashley Savain, Dr. Jan Bourne, Breno Vasconcellos, Eric Yang, Vincenzo Calcagno, Auria Robinson, Tori Chen, Brittany Reynolds, Benny Hurtado de Mendoza, Paola Lopez-Hernandez, Dr. Frank Muscarella, Ernst Ralph Pierre, Dr. Lourdes Canyamas, Dainely Fábregas, Teresa M., Rakesh Shah, Johania Charles, Keyonvis Bouie, Shania Rodriguez, Taylor Checkley, Mia Mcleod-Frederick, Lancy Clerveau, Mirko Ronchi, Cindy Luc, Jamila Gowdy, Fabrizio Montero, Matthew Ferrell, Shanovia Warren, Lisamar Perez, David Durham, Fatimah Lapin, Darrell Duvall, Lana Sumner-Borema, Julia Suglia,

Brian S., Brenda Hernandez, Marvin Best, Christa Jeanty, Alex Perez, John Boone, Amanda Traynor, Krystal Revel, Nia O'Connor, Claudine Destine, Wilhelm Karnbrock, Frantz Francois, Abigale Santiago, Victoria Martinez, Jimmy Cohen, Juan Cruz, Tracey Presume, Juan Gomez-Sanchez, Isabella Alvarez, Faith Acfalle, Dr. Lilia DiBello, Nelson Gonzalez, Nia Allen, Amine Maihouane, Amanda Gonzalez Garcia, Brandi Chisholm, Marika Thomas, Paris Razor, Denis Ordonez, Oriana Urdaneta, Lemiah Bates, Maxime Philius, Ninaliza Caba, Nils Vogt, Damian Campbell, Paola Melendez Reyes, Dai'Jonnai Smith, Steven Worthy, Faustino Yanes, Dr. James Haralambides, and Dr. Jill Farrell.

I am particularly grateful for the assistance provided by the Creator's Institute and New Degree Press staff, specifically Eric Koester, Mozelle Jordan, Erika Nichols-Frazer, Brian Bies, Jamie T., Heather Gomez, ChandaElaine Spurlock, Sherman Morrison, Haley Newlin, Kristy Carter, Emily VanderBent, Lyn S., Gjorgji Pejkovski, Milos Mandic, and Rodel Fariñas.